LOVE
INCORRUPTIBLE

A Woman's Reflective Journey to Freedom

Jazmin Steele

*To every woman and girl in the world – may you find your power,
believe in your worth and learn the art of putting yourself first.*

Backstory

As a child, I wanted to live like my white friends. You know—a good, normal life where Dad happily provided for the family and Mom packed lunches that included little loving notes and then prepared dinner at the end of a long day. In my eyes, white families appeared to have what black families did not: happiness. As a young girl, I yearned for my mother's love, and then I became angry at her inability to properly provide it. Our disconnect felt like awkward silence and lasted throughout most of my youth. On the other hand, my father was Superman and could do no wrong in my eyes, at least when I was a child. His efforts to put a smile on his little girl's face were far and few between, but they mattered—from carefully leading my first bike ride throughout our suburban middle-class neighborhood to building a makeshift swing set in the front yard of our home. For the most part, my parents gave me a good run through my grade school years.

By the time I was six years old, my fantasy of a normal family was thwarted by constant drama, drugs, and the overall despair between my parents. One day could be filled with carefree giggles and picnics at the park. By night, tension and the smell of cocaine residue filled our picture-perfect home. My parents' relational strife stacked like dominoes, tipped over, and began to dismantle. The verbal altercations increasingly ended up in black eyes for Carol. During their arguments, my younger sister, Cali, and I listened from our bedroom next door as our hearts pounded and teeth clenched, waiting for the screams to end.

Generational dysfunction was woven throughout my family's fabric. My mother, Carol, was born into a southern family in one of the poorest towns outside of Jackson, Mississippi. She was the youngest of eleven children and lived humbly in a two-bedroom apartment with her mother and father until he left. She grew up to become the beautiful cheerleader every boy wanted and every girl envied. As an adult, she suffered from the "me, me, me" syndrome that she'd acquired during childhood. I believe the exaggerated attention she received as the youngest sibling created a monster. She had issues of self-absorption and paired them with a passive-aggressive student-athlete, my father, Carter. They both clamored for attention.

Carter was the youngest of three, raised in a working middle-class family with both parents. I quickly realized that he didn't care much for any of his family; his father was the exception. The rest of them he couldn't care less about, and quite frankly, he talked mess about them all. "That broad didn't care about anyone but herself. She sold my car without telling me when I left for college. She never gave a shit about me." These were some of the statements about his mother that echoed throughout my upbringing. I'm positive that there was some childhood trauma he experienced that would justify his resentment, but I wasn't sure that he would ever be truthful enough to acknowledge it. He was known in the community for playing baseball, and unfortunately for my dad, that early-life popularity created a monstrous child-star syndrome in his adulthood. I often recalled him seeking approval and praise, demanding that others respect him. Whenever we brought someone new around, he constantly suggested the person "go look him up," as if he were some celebrity. He assumed everyone had already heard the worst about him. I saw my father as a sad and resentful person blaming the world for his lack of success. He blamed the world for everything.

These two people made up my foundation. Unknowingly, their broken spirits transferred toxic baggage to their children. They were two of the countless parents who committed this offense toward their children every single day. Our household was no different. The resentment from their childhoods planted seeds into the core of my being, shaping me into an emotionally shattered and insecure child. I questioned my worth and developed my very own childhood resentment. I had become my parents.

Then one day I woke up …

"THE CHILDHOOD SHOWS THE (WO) MAN, AS MORNING SHOWS THE DAY."

– John Milton

Chapter 1

My Genesis

The childhood shows the (wo)man, as the morning shows the day.
—John Milton

When I was around seven years old, my parents, Carter and Carol, realized that their toxic relationship would no longer work, and they parted ways. My younger sister, Cali, and I began court-ordered visitation with our father shortly afterward. All the family changes felt very confusing to me, but I typically remained quiet and absorbed all the negative emotions happening around me. During one of our evening drop-offs in the parking lot of a nearby Ralph's Grocery Store, my parents engaged in a predictable jealousy-driven argument. Like clockwork, my palms began to sweat and my teeth gritted as a subconscious reaction to the fear of God that Carter had put inside me. Their voices grew louder and louder.

"Bitch, get out the car and say that shit to my face!" he yelled.

My bladder tightened as I sat in the front seat of my mother's rust-colored 1980s Honda hatchback. I felt at any given moment my mother would be dragged in the parking lot in front of the rush hour crowd and I would pee on myself.

"No, Carter. Not in front of the kids! Stop it, damn it!" my mother pleaded from the driver's seat at a flailing Carter, but he did not yield. "I am going to call the police!"

Before I knew it, my father seemingly had a nostalgic moment of his glory days, and he power pitched my backpack into the front windshield, shattering the glass.

"Daddy, please stop! You are scaring me!" I pleaded as I witnessed a demonic spirit take control of his body.

My screams continued, hoping that the sound of his little angel's voice would end his rage, but my voice didn't matter at the time. His desire to provoke my mother outweighed my fearful cries. Bystanders walked in and out of the grocery store with looks of shock on their faces and reluctance to help. Their gasps and whispers added insult to injury in an already embarrassing situation. I sat there wondering, *Why the heck aren't they helping us?* As if the responsibility fell on a complete stranger to save us from what felt like a never-ending tantrum from my father.

In a lucky instant, my mother managed to scurry off and cut out of the parking lot without hitting anyone with our rickety hatchback. Our moans of despair filled the car, and we escaped the madman dressed as my father. He went so far as to chase us on foot.

"Hurry, Mommy, hurry! Please get us out of here," begged Cali from the back seat.

"It's okay, honey. We are okay. I'm so sorry," my emotionally beaten mother replied.

Why did my dad continually act out in such violent ways—and in front of his children? My fear of him increased as I witnessed each angry incident over the years. This scene was by far one of the most poignant.

Another mad moment took place when I visited my "uncle" Maurice— he and his wife, my mother's best friend, were longtime acquaintances of our family. He wasn't a biological uncle, but nonetheless he played that role. Their daughter, Ashlee, was my "cousin," and we shared a close bond. We played regularly on weekends, attended each other's birthday parties, and did family camping trips and magical weekends at Disneyland. These people were truly our family. Shortly after my parents split, my mom started to date this "uncle," and within a few years, she married him. Yeah, some real Jerry Springer mess. It's kind of difficult to justify marrying your best friend's ex-husband, but it happened. Their union created tension between all parties, but we children managed to maintain our love for one another throughout the years.

On this particular afternoon, I was supposed to be visiting my dad per the court order, but Carol changed the plans without properly notifying him. Once Carter Sapphire caught wind that I was over at Uncle Maurice's house, the end of the world commenced. Maurice picked up Ashlee and me from school; we were the same age and even sat in the same class. We played with our Barbies on the living room floor of their two-bedroom apartment. The apartment was nestled in the cul-de-sac of a lower-middle-class neighborhood. All the rooms were painted a shade of pale gray, with very few family photos scattered about, creating a feeling of detachment when one walked in. On this day, Tom and Jerry cartoons blared in the background as Uncle Maurice threw together some cold cuts for all of us.

"You girls ready to eat?" Maurice began, but he was cut off by hysterical banging on the front door.

A monsoon didn't compare to the frightening pound on that door. Ashlee and I dropped our Barbies and quickly scooted near each other. We waited to see who the crazy banger was on the other side.

"Who is it?" Maurice nervously inquired. He looked out of the small window to the right of the door.

To his surprise, there stood an irate Carter yelling at the top of his lungs. "Open this door, fool! I'mma beat yo' ass!" He banged on the door some more. "Gimme my goddamned daughter!"

Maurice frantically tried to secure the door, but he failed to pull the chain across the top in time. "Man, please, don't! Don't do this!" he pleaded as Carter wrestled with the door to remove it from the frame.

In true SWAT form, Carter kicked in the door, tossed it out of the way, and pounced on Maurice like a lion prepared to feast. Maurice attempted to guard himself using involuntary defensive tactics, but the flurry of blows to his body and head were unstoppable. It felt like time froze as Ashlee and I watched our fathers' altercation.

"Get off me, man! Stop, please! Stop!" Maurice pleaded but was incapable of landing any solid punches in his own defense.

As the ass-whooping took place, Ashlee and I got out of the living room and ran straight to the bathroom, hoping to protect ourselves from what seemed like World War III.

"Daddy! Daddy! Please don't hurt my daddy!" shouted Ashlee.

I stood next to her, peering out of the bathroom door to make sure my dad wasn't the one losing. There was something protective about watching my father charge into Maurice's apartment like my very own Superman to save me. What he did was tragically wrong, but strangely, it brought me a sense of security in that moment. I felt empowered and powerless at the same time.

After my dad finished unleashing his pent-up rage on Maurice's face, he walked back to the bathroom, grabbed my hand, and led me safely out of the front door. "Let's get the hell outta here," he commanded.

I was being rescued, although I was completely terrified of the person holding my hand. I was shaking like a wet dog and hated the fact that I was leaving Ashlee behind. I remember looking back at her and feeling so sad. The last ten minutes in that apartment felt like someone hit the slow-motion button on a tape player, with the words distortedly screeching in my ears. Carter continued charging forward, dragging me to his two-door silver Porsche Boxer. He stuffed me in the back seat with my sister.

"Put your seat belts on," Carter stated in a winded voice. "Now, is everybody okay?"

Did he not realize what he'd just done? Were we okay? Hell, no, we weren't okay! My heart sank for the both of us. Things would have been much simpler had I been able to stay, eat my turkey sandwich, and continue playing Barbies on the living room floor. That would have been okay for me. As I grew older, this distorted view of men warped my life choices. What I didn't realize was that my father's violent ways fostered a deep-rooted sense of insecurity that would follow me into adulthood.

About two years later, when I was nine, there was another significant male figure who planted a distorted seed into my life: my cousin Kevin. Good ol' Kevin was loved by everyone, including me—well, a little too much by me. Six years my senior, Kevin had that chocolate fineness that all the girls creamed their panties over. His name was always plastered over the local newspaper with his football stats and achievements. Kevin was the man. He also was the man who found pleasure playing house with his younger cousin. As a nine-year-old, I was clever enough to find ways to sneak back into his Playboy poster–covered bedroom so that we could go under the covers and fondle. He wanted me to perform oral sex on him all the time, and I always hesitantly did. He would guide my head up and down as I emulated characters that I saw on television. I knew it was wrong, and it definitely felt awkward, but I continued to do it anyway. This went on for about a year.

Sneaking off to have our incestuous encounters helped me receive the attention and love that I needed so desperately from my father. The constant quarreling between my parents caused me to feel out of place, and I always looked for consistency and protection. Kevin was that for me. The crazy thing was that we never got caught. No one paid attention to us. The adults were always so wrapped up in their own conflicts and gossip that they rarely took a beat to check on us. The freedom we shared with each other, although extremely inappropriate, was exactly what my heart craved, and it kept me coming back for more.

Whenever he played a Ready for the World record or asked me to wear purple as an homage to Prince, it brought a taste in my mouth that was disagreeable yet sacred. Those songs represented the permanent stamp of our inappropriate love affair. I was nine, and that relationship would set off a ripple effect for years to come as I used male attention as an antidote for my endless need for love.

"I USED TO BE A PRINCESS...BUT I DRIFTED."

– Unknown

Chapter 2

Misguided Love

I used to be a princess ... but I drifted.
—unknown

I had a few other sexual experiences by the time I reached middle school, but my virginity was still intact. The quest for acceptance from peers had begun, and the feeling would only become more unquenchable. Becoming a serial liar, coupled with my already deep need to be liked, got me in big trouble, especially when I lied to myself.

"Yeah, I'm ready to do it. I'm ready to have sex," were the words I regretfully told my sexually active best friend Jax, the beautifully thin, 'round-the-way girl who attracted all the bad-ass boys. Jax was my school ditching partner, my boy-chasing road dawg, and my "all things teenagers should not do" partner in crime. She seemed mature, and I wanted to be like her. I wanted to be grown so badly, with my mini-size A-cup bra and acid-washed Bongo jeans.

"I know exactly who I want my first to be," I convincingly protested to Jax.

I *really* did not want this. My brokenness was controlling my words, and all I really needed was for someone to save me. Why was I forcing myself to do this? Why isn't someone whispering in my ear how valuable I am, and that twelve-year-olds don't have any business having sex?

Is my cherry going to bust? I will probably bleed everywhere. My vagina is going to feel like someone ripped it open! These thoughts raced through my head prior to my virginity-snatching ceremony. The very thought of someone laying on top of me and forcing themselves inside my body caused my heart to palpitate and palms to clam up. Here I stood, an innocent child on the brink of making an adult decision that could never be undone. Even though I was terrified, I was willing to go through this painful experience in order to receive a possible fraction of someone's love. That love would be counterfeit, but it'd temporarily fit for this hurt little girl.

On this sunny Friday afternoon, Jax and I raced home after school to clean up her entire house with a fine-tooth comb in preparation for the big moment. The house was parent free, and so we had unrestricted reign over the nicely kept four-bedroom digs. Most of Jax's neighbors were still working at the time, which made it a cakewalk for us to be there in the middle of the day. The doorbell rang, and Chauncey stood confidently in anticipation with his tall, athletic build and milk chocolate skin. His thug appeal was topped off with red Chuck Taylors, a white tee, sagging Levis, and silky cornrows that trailed down his back. I had officially fallen into the trap of the physically mesmerizing but emotionally unavailable gangsta type. His swag lacked nothing other than an education and a father figure.

"Aye, Jax, is she here?" he asked.

I miraculously tuned into his voice from down the hallway and awaited Jax's reply.

"Yes, she's ready for you," Jax said as she unlocked and twisted the knob on the door that would forever change my little life.

On this day, Chauncey, the eighteen-year-old man who would take my innocence, came ready for the job. After all, Jax had prepped him on my virgin status, and he jumped at the opportunity to take it from me. He walked down the hallway to Jax's bedroom as I lay there on her twin bed, trembling with fear. At no point in time did I think I had the power to change my mind or even vocalize it. I wasn't emotionally strong enough to say the word no, so I passively stayed quiet. God, how I wish I'd had the courage to say something.

"So, you ready for this?" Chauncey asked.

I didn't think he really cared. "Mmm hmm." I simultaneously clenched my lips and lied through them.

The thick cloud of discomfort gradually filled the room as I anticipated my fate. Chauncey walked toward me as I squeamishly slid under the NWA throw blanket on top of Jax's bed. He removed his shirt, unbuckle his pants, and pull out what looked like a third leg.

"Oh, damn!" slipped out of my mouth, and I could hear my poor little heart pounding in my ears. *Thump, thump. Thump, thump. Thump, thump!*

There was no conversation, and there was no turning back. I was muted, and my dignity was on its way out the window. The moment that should have been saved for my husband in another twenty years was being ripped from me in a damn setup to which I stupidly agreed. Chauncey climbed onto me and began to moderately penetrate. The pain of insertion kept me from holding still for the next ten to fifteen minutes. I slid around the bed left and right until he grew tired of chasing me.

"Wait. Okay, okay, you can go now. Okay, okay … no! Stop!" I pleaded while trying to woman up and endure the pain. After about another five minutes of stopping and going, he gave up. I was so relieved! I never wanted something to be over more in my entire life.

"Yeah, you talked a lot of shit, but you wasn't ready," taunted Chauncey as he disappointedly slid his clothes back on.

I sat in silence and embarrassingly snapped up my Guess jeans romper. We awkwardly shuffled out of Jax's room without a word to say to her, both disappointed in what had just gone down. We left out the front door one by one in silence, and then we walked off in opposite directions. I headed toward my house, about five miles down the thirteen-mile stretch of Skyline Drive, a busy street that cut through the center of our inner-city dwelling. The laughter of children hanging out after school and fast cars racing through traffic lights provided the background noise to my shameful plot. I was bleeding profusely in my underwear and felt like a rape victim. And to think I expected this to be a moment I would brag about. *Damn it, Jax!*

A few years went by before I got over the trauma of my first time. That was something that I swore I didn't want to feel ever again. However, the hiatus came to a halt when I met Tank, a grown man. One day as I enjoyed the freedom of my parental absence, I walked to my local convenience store to get out of the house and hopefully meet some guys. I was all alone. My wish came true, and Tank pulled up alongside me as I swished my tail down Skyline Drive.

"Hey, cutie, what's up?" he shouted from the car window.

9

Tank was twenty-three years old and drove a little yellow knock-around Hyundai. He had a car and a little money (more than I ever carried), which was enough for my standards. Most important, he seemed to be a man—a real man. Tank was just what the doctor ordered.

"Are you talking to me?" I coyly replied.

"Yeah, I am talking to you. Bring yo' ass over here," he commanded.

The disrespect didn't bother me; after all, what self-worth did I truly have? After we exchanged a few moments of banter, without hesitation I jumped into a complete stranger's car with no regard for my own personal safety.

"Where are you headed, pretty lady?" he inquired.

"I was just walking home. Can you drop me off?"

"Yeah," he casually answered.

I excitedly rode in the passenger seat as he laid his hand on my young, tender thigh. The chemistry between us was immediate, and I was subconsciously pursing my next quest for love. He was one lucky guy because he wouldn't have to work very hard to get what I'm sure he ultimately wanted from me.

"You can drop me off right here," I said to him as we approached the corner of Skyline and Los Alamos. I wasn't crazy enough to show him exactly where I laid my head at night. "You want my number?"

"What you think? I ain't writin' my number down for no reason, so make sure you use it," he said.

Prior to exiting the car, I smiled at Tank and gave him a strong indication that I'd be calling sooner rather than later. I stared at his phone number all night long, imagining what this new relationship would look like. I was young, naïve, and totally jumping the gun on this relationship. I didn't even know his actual name. The fact remained that my father still wasn't around, and my void still needed to be filled.

During our courtship, Tank exposed me to the life of drugs, pimping, and prostitution. Although I never participated in the lifestyle myself, I was around it enough to be affected by it. Like most fatherless daughters, I fell victim to living life on the edge in hopes of gaining some value in it all. Tank used to pick me up most days from my neighborhood high school, Samuel F. B. Morse, one of the two most popular, predominately black high schools in San Diego; it was about three miles from my home.

Typically, we would smoke weed in his car and go back to his house—excuse me, his mother's house—to have sex.

One Friday afternoon, I snuck out of school at lunchtime after receiving a message on my cell phone from Tank that he wanted to pick me up. I always enjoyed spontaneous pickups from him because it made me feel special. I felt important that a grown man wanted to be with me. My vulnerable ass always jumped at the opportunity. While all the other girls chased around simple high school boys, I was well on my way being courted by a man.

"My high is coming down. You wanna get something to eat? I feel like some Wendy's," Tank suggested.

I had no opinion and simply wanted to go with the flow. "I don't care," I thoughtlessly replied.

My lack of self-worth showed in the simplest of things. The goal with Tank was to always be compliant and never to rock the boat, because doing so would jeopardize the "love" and attention that I received from him. The more I remained passive, the more I felt in control of what I received from him. It was pretty twisted.

As we headed to grab a bite, he mentioned needing to make a stop at his house, which wasn't out of the norm. However, this time something different happened. Tank introduced me to his mother.

"All right, we are gonna be in and out," he assured me.

Smelling like weed and french fries, we fumbled into the front door of their freshly manicured two-story brick home in Paradise Hills, a middle-class neighborhood a few miles away from the Skyline area where I lived. We hoped to get straight to his bedroom without any interruptions, but that was an epic fail.

"Oh, hey, Mom. This is my friend Brooklen," Tank said.

One of her eyebrows raised, and her head tilted downward like a teacher preparing to scold a student. "Brooklen," she uttered.

"Hello, ma'am," I nervously replied.

I spoke like a child who'd been caught red-handed stealing from a convenience store. My face became flushed as she locked eyes with me.

"Come on," Tank commanded as he grabbed my hand to lead me into his room.

I was a child, but I knew this relationship was out of line. Still, filling my emotional voids took precedence over what was right. Even after that moment of embarrassment with his mother, we continued the relationship.

Later that night, as the hustlers, pimps, and hoes began to flood the Skyline streets for business, Tank and I rode through the neighborhood to make a few stops. I simply posed as arm candy most of the time that I spent with him. We pulled up to a little white house in the heart of the Encanto, a pocket neighborhood where mostly druggies and drug dealers dwelled. The house was an older property with an eerie stench, and consequently it served as a place to house prostitutes.

"How long are we going to be here?" I nervously asked as I walked up the gravel driveway, tightly stuffing my hands into the pockets my East Coast–styled puffy coat. "Brr," I complained.

"Just chill," he commanded. I assumed my position as the tagalong and shut up. We marched up the stairs leading to the front door, and Tank boldly walked through as if he lived there. "Hey, man, what up?" he greeted a very handsome and tall man with long, curly hair and blinding pearly whites. He almost looked like Jesus with a street edge.

"What up, my dude?" the man replied, and they briefly hugged. "Let me get back to this business." He disappeared into the hallway bathroom of the disturbingly cluttered house.

Tank proceeded toward the kitchenette to make a phone call. I grabbed a seat on the worn-down sofa near the front door. All of a sudden, from the bathroom I heard a woman scream.

"Ah! Daddy, please stop!"

There was a silent pause in the interaction between Tank's friend and the woman. It was just enough time for me to readjust myself on the edge of the sofa and lean in a little closer to get a better listen on the action.

"No, I gave you all of the money! I wouldn't lie, Daddy. Please don't!" the woman screeched, pleading like a slave as the man beat her.

I quickly nestled back into the corner of the couch, grabbing my purse tightly as if it would save me. Was he going to kill her? I discreetly peeked down the hallway from my seat, wanting to help, but I knew that I couldn't get involved in pimp and hoe business. I had to stay in my place. Tank obliviously continued his phone call while this poor woman was getting slapped around due to some financial discrepancy with her pimp. *What in the hell am I doing here? Why am I even sitting in a place like this?* I began to question my entire life as I sat in fear on the grungy couch.

"Tank, how much longer will we be here? I need to get home, you know? My grandmother is going to be worried."

Tank looked up from his phone and gave me the glare of death. If looks could kill. "Look, bitch, I said I needed to handle some business. When you roll with me, then you roll with me. So chill!" he shouted.

My heart dropped. The realization that I was possibly no better to him than that woman in the bathroom was a blow to the gut. For a moment, I sat on that couch feeling somewhat privileged because I wasn't the one getting my ass beat, but that thought was quickly checked. Was I really any better than her? We were probably more alike than I imagined. Shit, we were both being used by pimps, whether it was for money or free sex. We both seemed to be camouflaging our pain by tolerating abusive men and indulging in fleeting escapades. I sat there like a living, breathing oxymoron. That hoe was me, and I was that hoe—simple as that.

Tank finally signaled for me to get up so that we could leave. Shaken by what I had witnessed, I timidly asked Tank to take me home for the second time. The fear to disappoint him was battling my instincts. The drive back to Los Alamos Drive was disheartening for me. I could have been raped, beaten, or even killed! And even though I felt invincible like most teenagers, I also felt vulnerable and weak. Needless to say, I began to slowly consider leaving this dangerous pimp alone, and eventually I did.

Each and every tainted encounter that I had with a man dug a deeper hole into the fiber of my being. Another layer of my self-esteem was removed every time a male added a notch to his belt at my expense. If only my dad would have known the damage he would cause by leaving. Maybe, just maybe, he would have fought a little harder for me. Tank served as one of my many examples of dysfunctional love as I pummeled through my teens seeking approval and acceptance. Like a thief in the night, Tank came in and out of my life, leaving a permanent scar on my vulnerable heart.

"A GIRL WITHOUT A MOTHER IS LIKE A MOUNTAIN WITH NO PATHS; A GIRL WITHOUT A FATHER IS LIKE A MOUNTAIN WITH NO STREAMS."

— Kurdish Proverb

Chapter 3

The Broken Village

A girl without a mother is like a mountain with no paths; a
girl without a father is like a mountain with no streams.
—Kurdish proverb

T he freedom I had as a teenager would have been any kid's dream.
I remembered looking at friends with parents, rules, and curfews,
and I felt envious that they had someone who cared. A lot of times, Cali
and I would come home from school not knowing whether Carol would
even come home that night. We'd go into the kitchen and search through
what we already knew were barren cabinets, just to end up warming some
top ramen, or cutting potatoes into french fries without the condiments.
I don't know why, but we always seemed to have a bag of potatoes in the
house. After a while, it was second nature to drink tap water and scrape for
food. Then my mother would magically appear, seemingly refreshed from
her getaway and acting as if nothing happened. This passive-aggressive
behavior confused Cali and me. What was a good mother supposed to be
like? I remembered always feeling guilty and angry. I was angry that this
was my life and that others seemed to have it so much better than I did. I
felt guilty for lacking sympathy for my sick mother, like my sister always
did. I lost respect for her, and I felt she had become the source of my anger.

"I think I hear Mom trying to come through the front door," Cali
anxiously stated.

We were getting ready for school on a gloomy Monday morning, and like clockwork, our mother scrabbled around to stick her keys in the door of our dated, tiny cottage-like home on the west side of Skyline. The west side was safer than the east. We always wondered whether she'd show up on Mondays because the weekend was the time she disappeared.

"Ugh, I think it is her," I replied.

"Girls, where are you?" Carol said as she stumbled through our front door. "If you need me, I'll be in my room taking a nap." She walked down the hall to her room.

"If we need you? We always need you," I sarcastically stated.

I continued to brush my teeth in the sink of the single, tiny bathroom that we all shared, feeling annoyed by her comment. The cold, wet tile pressed against my feet. I had taken a shower, and Carol walked in behind me. By the time I was a teenager, Carol had created such an emotional disconnect between us that the thought of looking her in the eye irritated me. I loved her, but the drug demon had turned her into a person that I wanted nothing to do with.

"What did you say?" Carol asked in a pissed-off tone. "I'm sick of your mouth, Brooklen. I don't care how you feel about me, but you won't disrespect me!" I gargled, spit, and rolled my eyes in complete irreverence to her. "I'm talking to you, little girl!" she shouted behind me while simultaneously slapping the back of my head in an effort to get my attention.

"Bitch, don't you ever touch me!" was my thoughtless response to the woman who had birthed me.

I couldn't believe I had blurted those words! Most children fear their parents, but in this case, I loathed her. Well, I loathed her lack of parenting. My mother and I spun out on the wet tile and landed in the bath tub as I defended myself against her.

"You guys, stop it! Leave her alone, Brooklen!" Cali shouted while running into the bathroom to deescalate our brawl. She always defended my mom, and I was always trying to punish my mom.

"Get off me!" I shouted as my mother came to her senses from attacking me and climbed out of the bathtub.

The resentment toward Carol was easily triggered by her attempts to mother me. Although I needed and wanted a mother, I wanted a consistent one, a real one! I simply didn't respect her lukewarm attempts to love me, and it showed. Many days, I would depressingly walk into our home pondering the things that made me so angry—namely, Carol. Sweet Cali processed the absence of our parents internally, but I was the opposite, exhibiting my pain outwardly in fits of rage or, in other instances, sleeping away the pain.

A few days after the brawl with my mom, I laid on my cold, twin bed in the desolate room that I shared with Cali. The carpet was old, shaggy, and a rusty shade of brown, further depressing our environment. The walls were cracked, and a lonely window overlooked our unkempt backyard. I felt my body drifting into a slumber as I began dreaming of my six-year-old self …

"Hey, Daddy, where are we going?" I asked as we rode through the eclectic, urban neighborhood of North Park, where he shared a one-bedroom duplex home with his wife, Gloria, the petite Caribbean woman who'd stolen his heart.

"Oh, just wait, baby. Daddy has a surprise for you and Cali," he promised.

Cali and I sat in the back seat of his Porsche Boxer, grinning at one another in anticipation of the surprise. My dad rarely surprised us with anything other than his outbursts of rage. This time the surprise sounded like something that would put a smile on our faces. We drove through rush hour traffic and pulled in front of the small building where he lived. The sun shined on this perfect day as my dad moved forward the front driver's seat so that Cali and I could hop out. We joyfully skipped to the front door of his home in anticipation of the surprise. My father unlocked and pulled open the door to a sight that confused the shit out of me.

"Girls, meet your brother, Alonzo," Carter said.

Shocked and dumbfounded were just a couple of words that described the reaction to the existence of this child. This fool introduced us to what seemed to be a one-year-old baby, and he declared him our brother! What in the hell had just happened? I stared at the baby with my lips sealed tight, my heart pounding, and my brain swirling as to how something like this was even possible. At six years old, the only thing I kept saying to myself was, "My mom didn't have a baby, and so how is this my brother?" Cali and I looked at each other in disbelief.

"Are you girls excited to meet your brother?" Gloria asked in her Caribbean accent.

To be honest, I wasn't. I was confused. We continued standing in front of this little boy in silence. By the way, he was completely adorable. The Christmas music continued to play softly in the background because it was the holiday season, and the baby crawled around under the tree, looking up at us as if he was already in need of some sort of acceptance. The lights from the tree blurred in and out as I sorted out in my young mind what this all meant. I felt like I was in the Twilight Zone.

My dream abruptly ended when Cali woke me up. "Brooklen, you okay? You were mumbling in your sleep."

I woke up from my dream feeling the gut punch from the day I'd met Alonzo. My blood pressure skyrocketed as I jumped up out of bed and just ran out of the house. I don't know where the hell I was going. My emotions consumed me to a point of needing release. I ran toward a nearby park. I found a bench not filled with chewed-up gum and bird droppings, and I sat down. It took a few moments to catch my breath. Within moments, Tank came to mind. I slid my flip phone out of the pocket of my jeans and called him. I was hoping to find an escape and maybe even some comfort in drugs. Unfortunately (or fortunately), there was no answer on the receiving end.

"Just like I thought," I whispered in disappointment.

Tank wasn't there for me, just like all the other men who were in and out of my life. My expectations were all wrong. I inhaled deeply and reframed my thoughts as I watched the hood celebrities pass by in their old-school low riders. I listened to the carefree shrills of the neighborhood kids. The air grew cooler. My heart grew harder as I debated walking back home or staying at the park to avoid my reality. As usual, I set myself up for more disappointment and decided to sit and wait for Tank to call me back.

I sat.

And sat.

And sat.

The sun gradually disappeared behind the lavender skies. Tank never called me, and I pitifully made my way back to my cold twin bed on Los Alamos Drive. I seemed to always be waiting for love to come from another broken human being, and consequently I always left empty-handed. My echoing thought was if Carol and Carter would have known that their choices would have sent me into a life of all-consuming self-doubt and insecurity, maybe they would have chosen differently. This broken village set the foundation for all my future relationships. I would learn to give more than I received. I would try to fix that which was unfixable and tolerate the intolerable. Their poor choices were in direct correlation to my underlying discontentment and constant seeking of others' approval.

" ONE DAY, WE WILL ALL
FIND THE ONE THAT WILL
SHOW US WHAT LOVE IS
OR IS NOT. "

- *Jazmin Steele*

Chapter 4

Young Love Strikes

One day, we will all find the one who will show us what love is or is not.
—Jazmin Steele

By the time I was fifteen, I excessively drank alcohol, puffed on weed, and even smoked cigarettes that were saturated in embalming fluid (which could have killed me). My destructive life was leading nowhere fast. I engaged in sexual intercourse with grown men and disrespected my mother more often than I'd like to admit. Then one day, there entered the boy that would change my life forever.

Symone, an olive-skinned, petite, around-the-way girl was the friend who called all her male friends her brother, although she slept with most of them. That was her way of keeping them close, because she had to settle for the sister role due to the fact that none of them wanted her afterward. One day, Symone introduced me to her "brother" Xavier.

Xavier, also known as X, was the poster child for a bad boy, and he was a well-known gang member who had been kicked out of almost every public school in the city. He was the typical black male without a father, and he looked for his validation and manhood in the streets. What made him appealing, beyond the wounded puppy persona, was his charm. His deep chocolate skin, nicely groomed low haircut, and perfectly symmetrical smile were enough to keep any young girl's attention. After all, I was subconsciously looking for a daddy, and so the tough and protective image worked for me—or at least, I thought it did.

"Brooklen, meet Xavier, the guy I was telling you about," said Symone as Xavier and I locked eyes, grinned at one another, and shook hands. There was an unusual magnetism that transferred between us.

"Hey, how are you?" I cracked a smile on the outside, but I was like a giddy kid at Disneyland on the inside.

We briefly stood gazing at each other in front of Symone's small, family-filled home down the street from my always vacant home.

"You guys ready to go?" yelled Symone's mom, Cassie, a short and sassy, middle-aged woman with curlers in her hair.

We hopped into her gold Chevy Suburban to grab a bite. Xavier and I sat in the back row while Symone and Cassie sat in the front. Our close physical proximity was enough to get those endorphins ignited through the roof. Although there were minimal words exchanged, we could physically feel each other's energy. We tightly held hands and overlapped our legs on top of each other as Cassie drove toward the nearest fast food joint. This moment officially marked the beginning of our colorful love affair.

I immediately began ignoring all advances from new guys, and I ended any lingering affairs, Tank included. Like a knight in shining armor, X offered me everything I was looking for in a dad—excuse me, a male companion. He was likeable and funny, just like I remembered my dad being. He charmed any crowd. His personality was fluid enough to hang with the toughest drug dealers on the street, but he could sweet talk a chemistry teacher into giving him an A. X was a dream.

A few weeks later, we began having sexual relations, and it intensified our emotional attachments. He'd often say, "Our bodies are like a puzzle: they fit perfectly." I agreed. Xavier and I never fell short of experiencing ecstasy between the sheets. I was officially caught in his web.

Over the next few months, we spent many late nights falling asleep on the telephone and many days ditching school to spend time together. We were the perfect match: the bad boy caught the good girl. We did what most unsupervised teenagers from broken homes did: drank alcohol, did drugs, and had unprotected sex. We often made plans to gallivant around town in stolen cars and have sex on his bathroom floor while no one was home. My risky activities beat going to an empty, loveless, and parentless home. What kept me coming back for more was how X treated me like I was the only girl in the world. Everyone knew I was his girl, and I loved it. Shit, I felt mighty important being the girl to a popular football star who moonlighted as a thug after hours. He was the best of both worlds. All the girls in our neighborhood wanted him and hated me—and that was a part of the thrill. It felt good to be wanted.

On the other hand, X possessed a dark side that one would ever want to experience firsthand. I convinced myself that his fits of rage and violence were a sign of love. When he squeezed my arms to show me that he meant business, he also showed me that he cared. I would receive those incidents as acts of endearment and not control, fear, or abuse.

"Hey, Brook, can you pass me a cigarette?" Xavier asked as we sat on the tidy, leopard-printed couch in his family room.

X lived on the first floor of a moderately older condominium complex in the working-class neighborhood of National City. X was forced to travel to my side of town for school due to constantly being expelled for fights and having poor grades. He shared the condo with his mother and two older siblings, who were hardly ever home. On this particular evening, we'd picked up a couple of twenty-two-ounce bottles of Olde English 800 at the nearest mom-and-pop liquor store.

"Why do you smoke so many of those?" I questioned. "Nope, you don't need it. I'm not giving it to you," I firmly said as I kept my eyes glued to the special Friday night airing of *Nightmare on Elm Street*.

"What? Just toss me a fucking cigarette, please. Thank you," he demanded.

X smoked cigarettes like a veteran affected by post-traumatic stress, and I didn't particularly like it. I turned around on the couch and reached over to the nearby coffee table to remove his last cigarette out of the pack. I broke it in half and tossed it at him. "Here you go. Smoke that." Now, what possessed me to do that? I have no clue.

I immediately saw the angry demon come alive in his posture. His eyes resembled the same demon that I saw when my dad threw his tantrums years ago. "Ugh! What the fuck did you do that for?" he screamed. X brewed in his anger for only a few seconds. Then he walked about three paces out of the kitchen toward me as I kept my seat on the couch. In a blink of an eye, I saw his bottle of beer thrown directly at my head. The darkened piece of heavy glass flew swiftly past the left side of my head, hitting the wall behind me and falling next to the couch. I jumped up off the couch and headed toward the front door, hoping to escape the shattering glass and Xavier's wrath.

"Don't run from me now! You were bold enough to break my fucking cigarette!" Xavier shouted as he moved aggressively toward me.

"What in the hell are you doing?" I nervously asked, not knowing what would happen next.

I reverted into a child, reliving the violent spats that my father had once performed. X used both hands to push me against the front door, and my body slid down to the ground like a weighty carcass. My body trembled in fear on the wintry tiled floor for a few minutes. In a moment of clarity, I gained enough strength to get myself up, and I ran out of the front door.

X remorsefully followed me outside. "Brooklen, I'm so sorry! I don't know what came over me. Please, please forgive me," he pleaded as I sat with my head buried in my hands on the staircase outside of his condo.

I cried, wondering what this meant for our relationship. Why did he go from zero to a hundred on me like that? I mean, I guess I shouldn't have broken the cigarette, and then he wouldn't have become so angry. Maybe this was all my fault. The words, "It's okay, X," came out of my mouth as I rubbed my bruised arm and stared down at the concrete. "It's okay. I love you."

Xavier's violent episode spun me into a déjà vu of an incident when my father had punched a glass window at my mother's home when I was about eight. The shattered glass flew toward my mother and scratched the cornea of her right eye. The fear of God rose in me when I heard my mother scream at my dad's fist propelling through the front window. After all, at least the beer bottle that X tossed at me didn't actually make contact. *I guess what he did wasn't that bad, right?* Consequently, the invisible scar on my mind that day was much more devastating and long-lasting than any physical one.

During the first year of our courtship, on too many occasions I found myself not liking Xavier as a person. Rather, I loved his image and what he presented to the world. I didn't truly know the person who resided deep down underneath the damaged boy. He was a ticking time bomb, and that side of X ended up overshadowing the butterflies that I once felt for him.

Xavier's ongoing antics were becoming burdensome to the relationship. His constant groping of other females at parties, starting brawls at the drop of a dime, and even ditching me after basketball games to run with his friends were just some of the behaviors that caused me to lose interest. I started to seek something more, something different. My need for companionship and love yearned for something deeper, something gentle, and I was growing weary of walking on eggshells.

When I least expected it, an old friend reentered my life.

"THE UNLIKELIEST PEOPLE HARBOR HALOS BENEATH THEIR HATS."

— Author Unknown

Chapter 5

A Taste of Heaven

The unlikeliest people harbor halos beneath their hats.
—unknown

C harming, likeable, and focused summed up Ryan Best, my buddy from middle school. He and I shared a couple of classes together, and we always managed to lock eyes and exchange smiles throughout the halls of O'Farrell Middle School, the popular middle school that most neighbor kids attended. Ryan was a quiet guy who often got overlooked and placed in the friend zone by his female counterparts. His long, wavy hair was always neatly tied into a ponytail. He had a small but athletic frame, and his full-fledged Colgate smile would brighten up any grumpy person's day. On campus, this guy's presence lit up a room, and his personality lifted the spirits of students and teachers alike.

Our friendship during these short adolescent years never went beyond grabbing lunch together or working on school projects. Our friendship faded once we graduated middle school, and years would pass before Ryan and I met again.

On homecoming night of my junior year in high school, my bestie, Jax, and I made our way to a friend's after-party, which consisted of someone's uncle being the DJ, a hot and sweaty garage, hard liquor, and weed. I stood kitty-cornered next to the blaring music and tried to make out a familiar face coming my direction.

"Brooklen, is that you looking beautiful as ever?" Ryan Best complimented me as I stood like an urban model in my Guess jeans, bomber jacket, and burgundy lipstick with dark brown lip liner to make them look fuller.

I was caught off guard at the sight of him. Quite frankly, I was speechless.

"Damn, it's been a while. I mean, how you doin'?" He stepped closer toward me with the biggest grin as Tupac's "California Love" blared in the background of the overcrowded garage.

I could barely contain my excitement and bolted toward Ryan for the biggest hug. "Ryan Best!" I shouted his government name as I always jokingly did. We embraced for what seemed like forever in the crowd of onlookers. "I've wondered whether I would ever see you again."

We released our embrace and nestled into a corner for some privacy like a couple of canned sardines. "Looks like your wondering is over," he assured me.

The bass in the music continued to compete with our conversation while folks squeezed by us, whispering "excuse me" repeatedly. I scooted in closer to Ryan.

He said, "So, I heard through the grapevine that you and X called it quits."

It felt like the music skipped a beat long enough for the entire crowd to hear Ryan's question. I dropped my head, thinking about the breakup that still plagued me. Although my time with X had expired, the feelings of sadness still weighed heavy on me whenever his name was brought up. "Yeah, you heard right. Sometimes that's just the way the cookie crumbles."

Ryan lifted my chin up and looked me in the eyes. "You know you've always been my girl." I smiled. "I'm here for you, Brooklen."

In the moment, Ryan no longer seemed like he could only be the friend type that he was in middle school. This chance meeting rekindled our friendship, and the next few months evolved into what felt like heaven on earth. Ryan was the yin to my yang, the Obama to my Michelle, the Gayle to my Oprah, and the icy rain to my perfect storm. I had never experienced someone finishing my sentences, picking the boogers out of my nose, or even preparing a meal for me. Ryan showed me love in the most intense and indescribable way. We were homie-lover-friends. We had found a sense of true love in one another with no pain and no drama. Our connection was reserved for our understanding. We were two old souls in teenage bodies.

Our peers tried to guess it for months, but we denied our love affair in the hopes of keeping it private—and to keep Xavier from lashing out. We all went to school together, and so it was pretty difficult to hide, but we managed to swing it. Once we entered our senior year of high school, X had graduated and moved on, and we were able to let the cat out of the bag. After nearly a year of sneaking around town and laying my seat down flat on the passenger side of Ryan's midnight black 1995 Camaro, we were in the clear. The freedom was comparable to that of a caged animal that, after years of captivity, was released into the wild. Having to suppress my joy was more torture than I had felt as a child not having my father around. I was in the heartbeat of an experience that I longed for most of my life. I was ready to scream it from the mountaintops.

"Can you believe we are really doing this?" I said to Ryan as we shot the breeze in the front yard of his parents' home.

Ryan slid closer to me on the swinging bench that sat on the porch. We interlocked hands. "This is what love feels like," he responded without hesitation.

"I just want us to live in this dream forever. I can't wait to get out of the hood and really start to live our lives, you know?"

"That's exactly why we are going to go away. You're going to go to college to get savvy with business, and I'm goin' legit. We are going to be straight. Just wait." Ryan confidently proclaimed our future together almost daily. He was well beyond his years. He made me feel so secure, protected, and loved.

The Bests took me in as part of their family. They resided in a quaint, inner-city cottage blocks from our high school. Ryan's mother, Belle was a shit-talkin' New Yorker and homemaker. His father, Joseph, was a calm-spirited, yet firm, retired lieutenant colonel in the US Army. Along with Ryan's siblings, they lived a pretty stable and loving life. It was normal happenings in the Best household to receive daily home-cooked meals, washed and ironed clothes before school, and family time where the members exchanged healthy dialogue about school, politics, favorite foods, and crazy extended family members. This loving experience was new to me, and I found myself spending a lot of time with Ryan's family. Belle really filled in the gaps for me as a mother figure because Carol continued heavily with her drug habit throughout my high school years. Belle even went so far as to teach me how to prepare full-course meals, choose the best deals at the grocery store, and pull weeds out of a garden. She groomed me for the wife life. The Bests groomed me for family life.

Throughout my high school years, Cali and I had lived with our maternal grandmother, paternal aunt, maternal aunt, paternal grandfather, and various other friends and relatives. The climate of our lives was unstable and unpredictable, and I cried out for some type of normalcy. Ryan and his family were my new normal. Although I felt bad leaving my sister behind, truth be told, I was looking for a way out. Carol's drug binges were becoming more frequent, and our lives were moving on without her. I was tired of worrying whether she was dead or alive. I was tired of watching my grandmother scrape up the leftover dollars from our welfare check to buy us decent clothes and school supplies. Toward the end of my senior year of high school, my mother managed to show up at my grandmother's house long enough to drop off the surprisingly healthy baby she'd given birth to so that *we* could take care of him. Then she disappeared again. By the time I hit age seventeen, I felt thirty-seven. I was tired and desperately in need of a new life.

"How much longer before we get there?" I anxiously asked Ryan as he drove up the California coast on Highway 5. The wind blew softly against our faces in the convertible BMW we'd rented for our weekend getaway. The sun was beaming on a flawless seventy-five-degree day. There wasn't a cloud in the blue mass above us.

"Girl, just relax so you can be surprised," Ryan kindly insisted.

The new hip hop music craze from Northern California had made its way down to SoCal, and we were in love with the pounding beats, clever lyrics, and unique delivery of the rappers. We sang in unison to veteran rapper E-40; Ryan took the low notes, and I took the high ones. We were Bonnie and Clyde–ing our way up the highway and enjoying every ounce of our time together. Our connection was deeper than lust; it felt like my soul was interwoven with another soul, and the only way we could detach was death.

"Ryan, are you kidding me?" I shouted. "San Francisco? I can't believe you! What?" My voice crackled. The cool air of the Bay Area swept through the historic Golden Gate Bridge as we rapidly switched lanes. "Woo hoo!" I yelled through the open roof of our convertible.

My curly hair bounced against the summertime breeze, and Ryan periodically glanced at me. We spent the eight-hour car ride talking about opening a music store business and visiting college campuses that I could attend to earn my business degree. Then the phone rang.

"Hello?" Ryan answered.

"Ryan, are you driving? Pull over. There has been an accident. I don't know how to say this," explained Belle.

"Just spit it out, Mom," Ryan said.

"Ralph, he … he was murdered," Belle stated as she delivered the devastating news to her son.

Ralph and Ryan were best friends—two nuts off the same tree, cut from the same cloth. Ralph was a hustler. He could sell ice to an Eskimo. Apparently he'd sold a bad batch, and someone wanted his life for it.

"Wait. What the hell did you just say?" Ryan panicked. "Mom, wait. What?"

A startled Ryan entered into complete silence while Belle sobbed on the other end. Then the news began to register in his mind. More silence.

"No! No! No! Not my nigga Ralph," cried Ryan.

I nervously eavesdropped from the passenger seat and waited for an explanation. Without saying goodbye, Ryan hung up on his mother.

"What? What happened, Ryan? Tell me!" I demanded as Ryan's face grew pale.

He drove quietly, accelerated, and turned the vehicle around to head south. This moment would change Ryan, now and forevermore.

The drive back to SoCal felt like a bad dream. Ryan's closest friend was violently killed without warning. Did this really happen? It pained me to watch Ryan's uncontrollable tears, jolts of anger, and endless disbelief. The next couple of weeks unfortunately opened the door to more surprises.

"Ryan, get up, babe. You can't stay in the bed all day. We have that English exam today," I encouraged Ryan as he struggled to even brush his teeth from day to day.

"Nah, I'm good. Can you just see if Mrs. Q will send the test home with you? They know that we are together all the time." Ryan paused. On his face grew a look of heavy concern. He looked at me.

"What is it, Ry?" I asked.

"I don't know. I just have this eerie feeling. I can't explain it. I just don't feel right," he said. "I feel like I'm next."

I sat on the bed next to him to console him. "Don't say that. That's crazy. The people who got Ralph are long gone. I'm sure they are nowhere near the neighborhood," I assured the both of us.

"No. Ain't nobody worried about them fools. It's just a feeling in my gut. It's telling me something," Ryan insisted.

I struggled with watching him grieve the death of his friend. Now he was having his own feelings of death? I felt like I was living in the damn Twilight Zone. Life's positive flow was coming to a screeching halt with Ralph's passing and what seemed like Ryan's self-prophecies of death.

"Get some rest. I'll be back to check on you after my phone interview at Macy's. Stay in good spirits, my love. It's going to be all right," I encouraged him as I rose off the bed. With a heavy heart, I stroked his wavy hair and kissed his soft lips goodbye. With my backpack full of books and the weight of the world, I headed to school.

The day dragged, and I was anxious about my job interview. I was equally anxious about Ryan. I didn't like feeling any disconnect from him whatsoever, but I understood it. The seemingly uphill battle from grieving not only took a toll on him but affected me too. Ryan felt like my twin in an eerie way. When he felt something, so did I. I managed to push my way through the rest of the day before going home to dress for my job interview.

"Hey, Ry! Give me a call back as soon as you can. I nailed the Macy's interview. The lady seemed to love me. I'll be stacking those chips for us to get to the Bay Area in no time. Call me!" I excitedly said on his voice mail.

I drove my grandmother's 1994 sky-blue Ford Taurus home from downtown. As soon as I walked in, I smelled my grandmother's famous tamale pie, collard greens, and a pot of her late-afternoon coffee.

"Grandma, I did awesome on the interview!" I shouted as I kicked off my Cathy Jean platform heels near the front door. I tossed my pin-striped blazer coat on the arm of our sofa. "Very soon I will be able to help you out around here."

My grandmother shouted from the kitchen, "That's good to hear, baby. You're a go-getter, just like your momma. I'm sure they'll be calling you back."

My grandmother always found the time to encourage me. She was the rock of our family. She had birthed nine kids, lost two, and raised a handful of grandchildren. Her resilience was unmatched, and I saw nothing get her down. She had a solid five foot two frame with a strong Irish and Dakota Sioux Indian bloodline. She was Momma Madeline, and we called her M&M.

"Thank you, M&M. I'm about to hop in the shower. I left Ryan a message earlier. Could you let me know if he calls the house?"

"That boy is always calling this house, "she joked.

A long twelve hours had passed since the last time Ryan and I had communicated. No response after school. No response after my phone interview. I grew a bit worried and decided to finally lay down in my bed in hopes of getting some sleep. I tossed and turned for nearly an hour.

My heart dropped into the pit of my stomach when I heard the sound of my phone. I jumped out of a near-unconscious state and reached up to my headboard to grab my cell phone. Cali and I shared a room at my grandmother's. Cali lay sound asleep right next to me. I sat up and pressed the OK button in order to activate the light. Finally, Ryan sent a message.

"Hey, sorry I have been MIA. Been runnin' deals all day. About to go buy some car speakers with the Hawaiian dudes around the block. They got the hookup. Don't be mad at me 'cause I'm hustlin', baby!" I could hear his charming chuckle as I read the message. Gosh, that boy made my heart smile.

Ryan was a mover and shaker. He operated swiftly but quietly, and I admired him for being a businessman at such a young age. Although his choice of trade was frowned upon, he had dreams to turn his fortune into something legit, something big. He had dreams to make us rich. All our peers knew about his business skills, which meant there were haters lurking waiting for him to slip.

Minutes later, I responded to his text with a phone call. He answered. "Ry! Thank God! Where the hell you been?" I could tell the connection was pretty bad. "Never mind. Get the deal on the speakers, and let me know when you make it back home." Our call dropped.

Relieved, I rolled over and tucked myself back under the covers. I sent one last message. "And I love you."

The next morning, the sun peeked through my mini blinds as the smell of grits and bacon drew me out of a restful slumber. I immediately checked my phone. No messages. Ryan didn't even take a minute to send his goodnight text to me? That was strange. I quickly got dressed and headed out the door without even grabbing my grits and bacon. I hopped in M&M's car and headed to school with the main priority of seeing Ryan's face. Upon arrival, I ran into a couple of classmates.

"Hey, Brooklen, don't forget we are rehearsing after school for the Miss Morse Pageant."

"Damn. I totally forgot."

"Girl, this is important for your college applications. You'd better get it together," my classmate warned me.

I rolled my eyes at her. She had no clue about the mission I was on. "Well, I set up a second interview for a job this afternoon. Can you just let me know when the next one is? Please?" I gave a fake grin and walked away. I didn't have time for what felt at the time was nonsense.

I approached class with the nagging feeling that Ryan wouldn't be there. When I walked into English class, I scanned the room and found no Ryan. I sighed and continued toward a seat in the front of class to sit down. It felt like all fifty-four student eyeballs were staring me down. Once I sat down, my thoughts began to surge.

Maybe he just got caught up with some money-making deal, and the day flew by him? Maybe he is hung over somewhere from partying it up in some penthouse with half-naked chicks? Maybe he was kidnapped and being tortured somewhere? Maybe he was at home sleeping off the night before? The questions swirled through my mind. There really was no legitimate reason for him to go hours and hours without calling me. There just wasn't. My gut said something was wrong.

The after-school bell chimed. I had a small window of time to make it to my second interview at Macy's. After rushing to the bathroom to change clothes, I tossed my backpack in the trunk of M&M's car and headed out. As excited as I was to get a job and make some money, I was worried about my friend, my love. The taunting feeling of despair wouldn't leave me. I was still waiting for a message to appear on my phone, but no luck.

I survived my interview, and prior to driving home, I reached out to Belle to get an update. "Hi, Belle, it's Brooklen. How are you?"

"Oh, hey, Brook. I'm not doing too well. We haven't heard from Ryan, so we decided to go ahead and call the police."

What? My heart sank. I softly said goodbye, ended the call, and cried my eyes out in the parking lot of Macy's. Why in the hell was this happening? I mean, his best friend had just passed a few weeks prior, and we were all still grieving. I couldn't understand why my best friend was nowhere to be found. Was this some prank? Was his prophecy accurate?

The second night without Ryan came and went. When I woke up the next morning, I felt the onset of depression creeping in. I rolled out of bed like a woman in her third trimester of pregnancy, slow and uncomfortable. I didn't want to face the morning at all. Once dressed, I grabbed a slice of toast with some of M&M's homemade peach preserves. I encouraged myself out the door and onto school.

While I drove east on Skyline toward school, I glanced over to see police cars and yellow tape down in a canyon to the right of the road. I hesitated, as if I was going to make the sharp right turn onto the narrow dirt road to see what was going on. My spirit told me that Ryan was down there, but I kept on driving. Honestly, if Ryan was hurt—or even worse, dead—there's no way that I was prepared to receive that news.

A few minutes later, I arrived at school. I could imagine that my face looked like I'd just stepped out of a scene from *Paranormal Activity*. The bags under my eyes resembled dark storm clouds, and there was puffiness in my face due to the excessive crying. All I kept thinking was that my best friend was in that canyon and was alone, without me.

"What's up, Brook?" asked my classmate Kam, a friend of Ryan's.

"Hey, Kam. So you haven't heard?" I asked. "Ryan has been missing for two days."

"What? I haven't talked to the homie in a couple of days, but I didn't think anything of it."

"Well, he never goes more than a couple of hours without reaching out to me. Never. So something is not right."

Kam did his best to comfort me. "Well, damn, Brook. Keep your head up. I'm sure Ry is just hustlin' like always."

I remained dejected and worried about my best friend, my partner, and my lifesaver. The weight of the world sat on my shoulders as the spirit of Armageddon took place in my thoughts. I couldn't function, and so I left school early and headed to Ryan's.

I arrived less than ten minutes later to find hordes of people in the front yard and standing in the street. I sloppily parked the car, stepped out, and paused before approaching the house. My heartbeat audibly projected inside my ears like rapid fists punching a wall.

Everyone's voices sounded like the Charlie Brown teachers as I moved closer to the front door. My body was warm in anticipation of whatever news was about to come my way. While scanning the crowd, I spotted Xavier standing on the porch near the entrance of the Best residence. We looked at each other for a few seconds, but no words were exchanged. His eyes were red with drunkenness and possibly anger. I was aware that Xavier wasn't happy about my new relationship with Ryan, but I know he still respected Ryan and his hustle.

I entered the house to sounds of wailing and sobbing. I rushed directly back to his parent's room, and I was met with the sight of Mrs. Best, along with a few other family members, crying. Her face was covered in gut-wrenching tears.

"Brooklen, he's gone. They k-k-killed him," she murmured.

Time froze, and for a second I thought that I had died too. My eyes gradually rolled back into my head, and my knees buckled as I blacked out on Belle's bedroom floor. I drifted into a deep, dark, and dismal slumber.

Hours later, I came to. Belle had covered me in Ryan's favorite San Francisco 49ers blanket and tucked me neatly in his bed. She'd put on me one of Ryan's oversized white tees and a pair of his black Nike basketball shorts; apparently I'd peed myself as a result of fainting. Ironically, I was wearing exactly what Ryan wore the day he was murdered. Always my twin.

A few hours had passed since receiving the horrible news. It was dark inside his bedroom, and the hallway light crept in from under the door. Belle knocked and peeked her cute, silver-haired head in. "Are you awake, hon?" she inquired.

"Yes, I just woke up. What happened?" I asked.

Belle ran to console me as I began to cry.

"Why, Belle, Why?" I pleaded in gut-wrenching pain.

I had never experienced such an unexplainable pain. Literally, a piece of me was gone. I couldn't fathom life without Ryan. He and his family were everything I'd always needed. I craved what they gave me. They were the perfect to my picture, and now it was shattered forever.

Still sobbing, I said, "Belle, I can't do this. I just can't! My heart is tearing inside. What am I going to do?" I gave a piercing cry, like an eagle in the sky calling for her young.

Belle squeezed me tightly. I guarantee Belle felt it times a million. Then she whispered, "Baby, we are gonna get through this."

Forty-eight hours later, the two killers, ages sixteen and eighteen, turned themselves into the authorities. Why would they turn themselves in so quickly? I believed guilt began to eat away at them. These two selfish idiots stole my best friend's life for $200, a couple of dime sacks of marijuana, and a joyride in his new Camaro. Ryan was shot twice in the head. According to one of their testimonies, the first gunshot merely grazed his cheek, and he pleaded for his life. He even asked to be taken to the hospital. His plea was interrupted with the final and fatal shot to the back of the head. There was no trial because the two cowards plead guilty. They would serve the better part of their lives in jail while we were left to grieve the loss of one of the purest souls ever to grace the planet.

For the next few months, the agonizing pain I felt at losing my sense of security, losing my dream, and losing my best friend would be the fuel that drove me to finish our goal: move to the Bay Area and become rich. That was all we ever talked about. Ryan was my dreaming buddy. I decided to skip my high school prom, and a few weeks later, I graduated high school with honors and headed to Northern California to attend Cal State Hayward.

I continued to mourn his loss and stayed dedicated to our goal of getting out of the hood and living the good life. Ryan Best brought out the hustler in me. He left a beautiful tattooed statement on my heart that read, *Love lived here*, and it would follow me for years to come.

"EVERYTHING HAPPENS FOR A REASON."

- The World

Chapter 6

Life after Death

Everything happens for a reason.
—the world

My life-changing summer ended, and fall semester at California State University Hayward quickly arrived. Carter drove hundreds of miles up the coast and left me to a new life that included approximately fifteen thousand strangers, tons of cold rain, and the memory of the love of my life. I felt a mixture of excitement and guilt as I embarked upon the next phase of my life. On one hand, my heart melted that my father took time away from his current family to drive me up the interstate eight hours. That meant a lot considering we didn't have tons of positive memories. On the other hand, my heart couldn't take the fact that I was doing this without Ryan. I kept hearing his voice in my head say, "Hey, Lady"—a nickname that only he used—"you got this." He was my champ. Now, I knew it was time to be the champ for myself.

Back home, Carol checked into a fifty-two-week rehabilitation program. I believed the shock of Ryan's death put things in perspective for her. My sweet baby brother, the son Carol had surprised us with almost a year prior, Kanan, was now living with a family member while she attended rehab. Cali was becoming quite the track star and stayed with M&M to finish up high school. Everything at home seemed to settle down while I settled down into college life.

Loneliness struck as the excitement of the newness wore off. I had three fun-loving roommates who shared a spacious, on-campus, two-bedroom apartment with me. Being able to share my story with them brought some relief, but I knew those girls couldn't relate to me. They hadn't experienced constant death throughout their neighborhoods, abandonment, and loneliness in the way that I had. They knew none of it and only could offer an "I'm sorry" in the hopes of lifting my spirits and nursing my wounds. Like a zombie, I walked around the campus disconnected to the things happening around me. I was in my own bubble, and my unintentional isolation got the best of me. Feelings of desperation seeped through my skin like a bad odor, and it attracted the wrong people.

The solace I needed was answered by one of Hayward's notorious playboys. I didn't know who was who around town, so I was an easy target. All I knew was that I was wounded and looking for someone to help me feel whole again. Insert Tyrone. Now, Tyrone didn't even attend Hayward; he simply managed to loiter our apartment building in pursuit of his next piece of fresh meat. Unfortunately, I decided to ignore all the red flags upon meeting him. I recalled watching him from my apartment window as he conveniently slid into the front door of this chick's apartment across the way. She was a junior, and I was a freshman, so there was some intimidation there, but I was her competition. After all, he'd come to my apartment next.

Romping around with Tyrone for the next few months got me nowhere emotionally. I was startled after hearing and seeing news about the spread of HIV in the Bay Area. The nearby Oakland community was one of the fastest growing in HIV cases, and Tyrone lived there. The fear of God entered me as I imagined my life ending over some nasty-ass guy who couldn't keep his thing in his pants. I mean, the sex was amazing. Actually, I would go as far as to say it was the best that I'd experienced in my eighteen years. But it wasn't worth my life. I quickly terminated the relationship with Tyrone and regained my focus on the mission: to stay out of the hood and live the good life.

The first semester of college came to an end, and I survived it. The dark cloud I was battling started to dissipate, and I could see the light. I believed that Ryan was looking down on me with that ear-to-ear smile, saying, "You got this, Lady."

It was November 1998, and it was time to start packing up my things to go home for winter break. Out of the blue, I got a phone call from a familiar voice.

"Hello? Brooklen?" the voice stated. "Guess who?" It was Naomi, Xavier's mother.

"Naomi? Wow. It has been a long time. To what do I owe this pleasure?" I asked.

"Well, I had been praying for you and wanted to see how you were adjusting to school."

"I'm doing pretty good. I am actually packing my things as we speak to head home for winter break," I shared. "How's Xavier?"

"Funny that you ask. He wanted me to get your mailing address in Hayward. Do you mind?" Naomi inquired. "Xavier is in military boot camp and wanted to write you."

"Military? X? Are you serious? The last time we spoke, he was still gangbangin'," I boldly mentioned. "I'm shocked."

"Who are you telling, Brooklen?" she joked. "I prayed for the day that he would turn his life around. I am very proud of him. I will be flying to attend his graduation in the next couple of months. I can grab you a plane ticket, if you're open to coming."

"Well, thank you, but I don't know whether that is a good idea. X and I didn't end our relationship on the best of terms. I am definitely all right with him writing me. Let's start there," I bargained.

Butterflies rose in my stomach as I said goodbye to Naomi and hung up the phone. Xavier wanted to write me? The last time we'd interacted was centered on Ryan's death, and Lord knows that I wasn't in the best place emotionally to deal with X. Military? Now, that was a complete shocker, a complete 180. He must have done some growing up. I was open to taking a listen.

Maurice, who was now my stepdad, waited outside of my dormitory as I hugged my roommates goodbye for the break. We were all hopping into our cars to head to our respective homes away from the Bay. I was quite excited to see my hometown folk and felt accomplished to have made it halfway through my first year of college. I considered how things would be, going back to a place that represented so much pain. But once I touched the SoCal soil, the feeling of home hit me like a ton of bricks. I began crying tears of gratitude because I had survived so much.

We pulled up in Maurice's gold Toyota Camry to my grandmother's house. "Thank you so much, Maurice," I stated as he helped me unload my bags.

"Be good on break, girl," he uttered in his grouchy yet loving tone.

Maurice was a supportive stepfather. He really stepped in while Carol was away in rehab. He'd always be willing to make that long trip to get me from school or drop a few dollars in my bank account. Although times had been sketchy between him and my father, it didn't stop him from caring for me. I appreciated that.

M&M's yard was covered in purplish blue flowers from her Jacaranda tree. The six-foot bird of paradise plant looked exactly the same as it poked out into the driveway and scraped my shoulder when I walked by, just like when I was a kid.

"M&M, I'm back!" I shouted as I jumped onto her porch. She quickly made her way out and gave me a big bear hug. Gosh, it felt good to be *home*. "Cali, where you at, girl?" I shouted from the front door.

I spent a few moments catching up with M&M and Cali in the quaint living room filled with nostalgic photos and biblical scriptures plastered on the wall. My grandmother's house always had a strong sense of protection, and I felt safe there. As I gushed about my first semester at college, I was interrupted by a message on my cell phone from a familiar number.

"Excuse me, guys. Let me see who this could be."

I picked up the receiver of my grandmother's landline and dialed the number. I didn't want to burn up the minutes on my cell phone; I was on a broke college student budget.

"Yes, did someone message Brooklen?" I asked.

"Hi, Brooklyn. Yes, Xavier did. Hold on a second," offered Naomi

Those few seconds I waited were nerve wracking as hell. What was this going to be like?

"Brooklen! You there?"

My heart palpitated feverishly at the sound of his voice. "Hey, X. It's been a while," I softly replied to balance out his high energy. "What are you doing home? I thought you were away at boot camp?"

"Well, don't sound so happy to hear from me," he sarcastically noted. "I am here for the holidays. I was wondering if you would like to hook up, grab a bite or something."

I wasn't being sarcastic; I was protective. This guy had already broken my heart once. Once I let my guard down, I accepted his offer. "I think we can do that. This weekend works for me," I suggested.

"Cool. I will come get you Saturday night at seven. And, Brooklen, wear some comfortable clothes," Xavier added before we hung up the phone.

Was that a sexual reference? I wasn't sure. I paused to soak up the words that were just exchanged. *Could this mean we are getting back together? Where is this gonna really go? Wait. Stop it.*

My thoughts were cut off by an interjection from M&M. "Hey, baby, so tell me, how were those Bay Area folks?"

"Uh, yeah, they were cool, Grandma," I quickly replied in order to get back to my thoughts.

Over the next ten days, Xavier and I spent a large amount of time together. We went on dates to the movies and walked on the beach. I even had Christmas dinner with his family at Naomi's home. I was being inundated with X's pleas to take him back and his apologies for the way our relationship had ended. I had to admit that getting this kind of treatment from him was heartwarming, but I was reluctant. The primary reason I'd left him in high school was because I was tired of his immature antics that had caused me so much frustration. I always believed in my heart that X had more potential than he displayed. Was the timing lining up for the both of us?

"Xavier, I know the last few days we've been home together are moving pretty fast, like we didn't even skip a beat," I shared in the passenger seat of his 1999 Ford Explorer rental. "I don't know. Something about it feels right."

We sat parked on the beautiful tip of a cliff and stared at the pink skies at Sunset Cliffs Beach.

"I know. I've been thinking the same thing. I felt in high school that you were the best thing for me. I know I was a knucklehead and messed up a good thing," he nervously began. "I never mentioned to you how hurt I was when you and Ryan started messing around with each other." X frequently broke eye contact, looking at me and then the water.

"Yes. About that," I stated in my defense.

"No, no. Let me finish. I was hurt seeing you not only with another person, but with him. It was like a slap in the face to see you with someone I considered a friend," he explained. "Then I had to realize that I wasn't the boyfriend you deserved. I had to take that loss. But now, life has changed. I have changed, and if you're cool with it, I would like to give us another try." Xavier shared his truest thoughts, and his eyes settled on me.

I grabbed his hands. "Xavier, you know that I have been through a lot recently, between losing you and losing Ryan. I mean, he was my friend— my best friend. And for sure, I still love you. That's been obvious over this holiday break. I just—"

Xavier cut me off by placing his full, perfect lips on mine.

We kissed passionately in the front seat of the car while the crashing waves played as background music. Our lust for one another took over, and we ended up in the back seat. Our bubbling feelings took over, and we shared our bodies with one another in a passionate display of young love. We didn't care if anyone was watching; all we cared about in that moment was the reconnection of something that was once disconnected. The loneliness I had experienced the past few months in Hayward were redeemed in this very moment.

The holidays were over, and I reluctantly said my goodbyes to family, which included speaking to my mom over the telephone during her stay at the rehabilitation center, which was a few hours away from San Diego. Although quite broken, our relationship still had a pulse, and I made sure to show her respect regardless of our circumstance. Cali and I got to spend some much-needed sister time helping Grandmother cook meals and re-arrange her home for the holidays. The trip home couldn't have come at a better time. My need for family and reconnection filled my heart with a joy that had been missing.

"SOMETIMES, WHAT YOU'RE LOOKING FOR COMES WHEN YOU'RE NOT LOOKING AT ALL."

– Author Unknown

Chapter 7

Surprise!

Sometimes, what you're looking for comes when you're not looking at all.
—unknown

The Bay Area welcomed me back from the holiday break with open arms. My fun-spirited roommates gushed about their shenanigans during their time at home and how they couldn't wait to get back to the independence waiting at college. I shared about the rekindling of an old flame and how I was looking forward to getting to know him again through our plan to send letters. Considering all that I had been through, I was looking forward to a timely fresh start at the new year.

A few weeks into second semester at school, I discovered some unusual tenderness in my breast. Even putting on my bra was a task, and I attempted to avoid rubbing my nipples too hard for fear of agitating myself. I knew my body pretty well, and what I was experiencing was definitely out of the norm. I considered the thought of pregnancy only because X and I didn't use protection. At the same time, I couldn't fathom something like this happening to me. I was only eighteen years old, still a freshman in college, and I had all these dreams of beating the odds. These thoughts quickly spiraled, and I decided to go to the campus store and grab a pregnancy test.

I walked alone for fear of it being positive and having to explain to anyone else what was happening. I was so embarrassed checking out of the store. The glares from my fellow classmen were nothing short of judgmental. Truth be told, I'd be doing the same damn thing if the shoe was on someone else's foot. I snatched the paper bag with my fate in it and rushed back to my room. Thank goodness, no one was there. I rushed to the bathroom, did my thing on the stick, laid it on the sink, and prayed.

"Lord Jesus, I will never, ever have unprotected sex again! I am not ready for a child. I wouldn't know what to do with a child. Just please, please don't let this happen to me," I pleaded as two bright pink lines showed up right before my eyes.

"Positive," I mumbled as I slid down the bathroom wall, holding my life sentence in my hand—or so I thought.

I began to ball my eyes out into a puffy, pink disaster. Finally, I crawled off the floor with my head hung in disbelief. This could not be happening to me. January 7, 1999, marked another day that would permanently change my life. Was I ready? Did I want this? What about my dreams? Would I end up a failure? All these questions shot through my head like a machine gun spraying bullets.

Within moments of receiving my news, fear set in. I would become a teen mom and fulfill the life pattern of my family—the very thing that I wanted to avoid. Many of my female family members had babies as teens, never finished high school, and then went on to add more babies to their households than dollars in their bank accounts. Would I end up like them? Lord, No! The last thing on earth that I wanted was to live a mediocre life receiving welfare checks and food stamps. I mean, I had survived high school with little to no support from either parent. I'd escaped the streets of my neighborhood without getting addicted, pimped, or killed. I'd survived the death of my best friend, and I'd even earned myself a full academic scholarship. Considering all the facts, I was already beating the odds. But I was about to set myself back by having an unplanned baby.

Ironically, in my brokenness, I felt having my child was just what I needed. After experiencing such a painful loss and abandonment, it only made sense that God brought me back to life with this baby. That was my rationalization. I spent a few days weighing all my options, and notifying X that I was with his child was the next thing on my list.

"Hey, Brook, can I call you right back? We are getting ready to go do a quick drill," Xavier said on the other end of the phone.

"I'm pregnant," I blurted. I guess I wasted no time.

"Wait, what? Did you just say that you're pregnant? How is that possible?" Xavier asked. He already sounded like a damn man trying to escape responsibility. I was understanding of his shock. "I mean, I'm sorry. Wait. Wow, you're pregnant?"

"Yes. I took a couple of tests, and once my period didn't show up, I knew something was up." I paused before I stated my position. "And I don't want to kill the baby. I know, I know. We are young, and our lives are just taking off, but—"

"We are having a baby! We are freaking having a baby!" X shouted over the phone as my eyes welled up with tears. My fears of him being disappointed or angry with me didn't come true. He was okay with this. He really was okay? We were having a baby.

We notified our mothers because we expected to get the most support from them. To my surprise, my mother cried with joy and gave her full support. Naomi had always been a cheerleader of my relationship with her son, and she only wanted the best for us. She warned him, "If you mess around and disown this baby, then I will disown *you*." Naomi didn't play, and X decided that he would take seriously not only this new responsibility, but also his relationship with me.

A few months passed, and I finished up my final semester of freshman year in Hayward. Although there were positives to my college experience, I was never able to completely settle in mentally and emotionally. I was going back to my hometown to give birth to my first child, and my mind was on that business. Interestingly enough, I hadn't even told my biological father that I was pregnant yet. I was too scared. I decided to tell Maurice first because that was more like a baby step, and he was much easier to talk to. Maurice showed up to my campus on move-out day, as promised. Once I was all checked out, we started the eight-hour journey down south on the 5 Freeway to San Diego.

"So, Maurice, have you noticed anything different about me?"

"What, baby? No, why?"

"Well, if you look closely, you can tell that I'm carrying a baby," I shyly revealed.

Maurice took a beat to swallow that pill. "Well, does your Mom know?"

"She and Naomi were the first people we told. They were happy," I reassured him.

Maurice cracked a smile. "Well, I'm happy too. Congrats, baby," Maurice always supported me. "But you gonna need a job!" he joked.

After we shared a few laughs, I began drifting into thought about the days ahead. I was eighteen and was about to have a baby. Would people be disappointed in me? I envisioned all the judgmental faces of my family members. I could hear them taunting, "I knew you'd be back. You ain't no different than us." I heard the voices of friends wondering how I could have a baby so soon, given that Ryan's death had not even been a year prior. I even imagined how disappointed Ryan's parents would be. I feared their disappointment more than my own parents.

"Wake up, Brook. We are home." Maurice softly shook me out of my deep slumber. "I went ahead and brought you straight to Ryan's parents' home."

It was time to face the music. I definitely wanted to check the big things off my list first. Sharing my pregnancy with the people who had been my parents and mentors was no easy feat. Plus, I'd dated their son! Unfortunately, I had worked myself up with the fear of Joseph and Belle's reaction. They totally surprised me by showering me with the love that I needed.

"Brooklen, we know you loved our son, and our son loved you. We would have wanted to see you two have children," she encouraged me. "But we realize that life had other plans for all of us."

Belle's support filled my soul. I respected her and the Best family. The last thing I ever wanted to do was add more pain to this family.

"We love you, and congratulations," shared Joseph, who was a man of few words.

I continued my rounds, visiting family to tell everyone the news. I felt the weight on my shoulders being lifted every time I shared my story. Every time, I was being convinced of my own truth. Later that day, I had to stand the firmest in my truth when I went to tell my dad. By this time, he had already been living back in San Diego from Florida for a couple of years, and we communicated a few times a month while I was away at school.

Xavier and I arrived at the front door of Carter's residence. I stood there with sweaty palms as my heart pounded through my chest. I rang the doorbell.

"Brooklen! Xavier!" shouted Gloria in her Caribbean accent. "Well, don't just stand there—come on in."

We marched slowly through door as I anxiously concealed my belly. I found a spot on the couch in their neatly kept townhome, and like dominoes, we sat down one after another. Gloria prepared some beverages as we sat there counting the moments to drop this bomb.

"So, Brook, you finished your first year of college. You are on your way! And just like I said, time is flying by," he stated in his *I told you* so tone. "Xavier, how's the military?"

"Yes, Mr. Sapphire. I finished boot camp at the top of my class and just found out that I will be stationed on a ship right here at home."

"That's good to hear, son. Looks like you made a good decision to leave the streets alone and start a career."

Oh shoot. There was the judgment and condescension that I was afraid of. Awkward silence filled the living room.

"Well, Dad, we were making our rounds and wanted to make sure that we informed you in person of our news …"

I began to set up the knockout punch, but Gloria blurts out in her annoying voice, "Oh, no, ya pregnant?"

Gloria stood to her feet in anticipation of my answer while Carter stared a gaping hole through Xavier's face. Both of them could tell by the look on my face that Gloria was right.

"Well, how far along are you?" asked Dad.

"I'm six months," I replied.

"What in the hell? And you are just now telling us?" shouted my father. "Why didn't you say something sooner? We could have at least made you an appointment."

My father reacted exactly as expected. His rage from my childhood days was seeping through as he sat across from Xavier and me in his favorite, burnt orange antique chair. Carter thought everything he kept over ten years was an antique, when in reality the shit was just old.

"Appointment for what? We are having a baby," I confidently stated. I was offended by his assumption that I would want to kill my child. "Xavier and I have a plan, and we are going to be just fine. Don't worry. We won't need anything from you."

"Well, you sure sound like you know what you're getting yourself into. Let me ask you this: what happens if Xavier gets stationed across the country or finds another woman, and he leaves you to take care of this baby alone?" Carter argued.

I thought this was a pretty bold statement to suggest in front of our faces, but I wasn't the least bit surprised. He always thought the worse.

"Mr. Sapphire, I assure you that I love your daughter. I know that we are young and things can change down the road, but for now, we have a plan. We have a plan to be responsible and have this chi—"

"Y'know, I had a girlfriend who traveled a couple of hours north to get an abortion. I think you can get them done up to seven months," Gloria disgustingly suggested.

And at that point, I mentally checked out. Time to go. "You know what, Dad? I knew this would be the reaction from the both of you, which is exactly why I waited until I was six months pregnant to tell you. There is no way that I would murder the child that I have bonded with over the last few months. I've cried just listening to her heartbeat. Yes, *her* heartbeat. You are having a granddaughter. I've gotta get the hell out of here."

I stormed out of the front door with X trailing right behind. That didn't go so well, but I knew it wouldn't.

"Goodbye, Mr. and Mrs. Sapphire," Xavier whispered as we darted out of the front door.

As those two tried their best to persuade me not to have my child, they only pushed me further into wanting to have her and be successful. Their doubt motivated me to prove them and the world wrong. Shit, I knew that I could be a great parent—better than the two God had given me—and *still* complete college. Cal State University, Hayward, was where I'd started, but it wouldn't be where I would finish.

"GET UP, DRESS UP,
SHOW UP AND
NEVER GIVE UP."

- Genevieve Rhode

Chapter 8

The Real World

Get up, dress up, show up and never give up.
—Genevieve Rhode

My college dream with Ryan had been deferred by death and birth. The life I'd once imagined was no longer going to happen. I decided that I would chase new dreams. A few months later, Tyler Victoria was born. My baby girl. She was the tiniest ball of wonder that I had ever witnessed. As I marveled in her glory, I immediately connected to my motherly instincts. I knew without a shadow of a doubt that this brown-skinned, curly-haired being would catapult me into the life we both deserved. She deserved more, and I was willing to give it all to her.

As I adjusted to being a young mother, my thoughts got the best of me. Between breastfeeding and looking up classes to start my sophomore year back home, I battled a mild depression. As much as I tried to avoid becoming a piece of data like the examples I'd had growing up, I had to swallow the ugly truth that I was now a "black teen mother." The chances of me graduating college, becoming married, or being financially independent and successful had drastically plummeted. In addition, the likelihood that I would have another baby, end up on welfare, and drop out of college were even greater. These months were some of the toughest in my eighteen-year old life simply because I didn't have time to cry about it. I had to get up, dress up, and show up!

Back on my grind, I enrolled in Grossmont Community College, about half an hour east from the home that I shared with my mother. Carol had completed her twelve-month program and was drug free. We shared a home with Maurice, Cali, Ashlee, and my daughter.

My ultimate goal, as I crisscrossed that college campus, was to become successful and beat the odds. Instead of becoming a victim and succumbing to the pressures of generational curses, I decided to fuel my pursuit with the vision of my future. I realized that some dreams died, but others came alive.

On a spring day in 2000, my English teacher, a distinguished American man with a love for all people, gestured for me to speak with him after class. "Brooklen, you are doing a wonderful job in my course. I loved your take on Ernest Hemingway's *A Farewell to Arms*," he complimented. "Let me ask you something. Have you ever considered attending the prestigious private school, the University of San Diego?"

I shook my head in a pure state of confusion. "Uh, no. Why would I ever consider going there? Isn't that for rich kids?" I ignorantly asked.

"Well, yes, children who come from wealthy homes do attend. But I am a part of the diversity team at the university, and my sole purpose is to help bring some, shall I say, color to the school," he casually explained. "Look, Brooklen. I believe in you. I know your story, and you've had some tough breaks, but I don't think those things determine your future. Your future is up to the choices that you make today. Do you believe that?"

"Well, yes. I do believe that," I stated. "But how in the world could someone like me get into a school like that?"

"You just leave that up to me. Keep up the great work here at Grossmont, and I will schedule a tour for you and a few other students to visit the University of San Diego. You'll be able to see, feel, and smell the atmosphere on campus. My feeling is that you will see the prestige and find that it matches the prestige that lies in you," he encouraged.

My heart nearly jumped out of my chest after meeting with my professor. The University of San Diego had one of the top business and law schools in the country. Surely only the wealthy could afford to send their kids there. Someone with my background would be forced to take out loans to obtain that six-figure education. Thankfully, my professor saw something that no one else seemed to share with me up until this point.

He saw potential. He believed in me, and it was time that I began to believe in me too.

At the end of summer 2001, I finished up my general education at Grossmont Community College. With my hard work and a letter of recommendation from my English professor, I landed a spot on the University of San Diego campus as a junior. There was a whole new world of opportunity at my fingertips. The people were different than those I had associated with in the hood. These people came from different cultural backgrounds, spoke different languages, and even walked differently! And I was now one of them. The only thing that separated me from them was what went on between my two ears. If I kept telling myself that I was only a black teen mother, then that was all I'd ever be. I had to start thinking differently, dreaming bigger, and expanding my circle of friends.

I spent the next two years focused on school and my family. Honestly, I didn't have much time to do anything else. While Xavier managed to move up rank in the military, I maintained above a 3.0 GPA and made the dean's list. Together, we were young parents doing the "right" thing. My goal to stick things out outweighed the relational struggle. I'd had many dreams halted, but the dream of creating the family that I always wanted remained a top priority.

Wow, I really did it. Graduation was around the corner, and I was getting ready to walk into the light at the end of the tunnel. I would become the first person in my immediate family and my generation to graduate with a college degree. The battle to push away negative thinking was ongoing, but it didn't stop my dreams from unfolding right before my eyes. Tyler Victoria would get to cheer her mommy on as I walked across that distinguished stage against all odds. With a lot of hard work and family support, my dream to graduate college was realized. The time it took me to earn my bachelor's degree came with many days and nights of sacrifice. Holding that piece of paper in my hand made it all worth it.

"Brooklen Sapphire," stated the President of the University of San Diego. "Receiving a bachelor's of science in business administration with an emphasis in marketing." Those words resonated with me so deeply. Those words changed me.

Unfortunately, basking in my success was short-lived because of the looming issues in my relationship with Xavier. We were both twentysomethings trying to figure out who we were and how to raise our daughter at the same time. In the following years after Tyler's birth, we both did our share of cheating and breaching of trust. It was virtually impossible to know how to conduct ourselves properly within our relationship because of our lack of successful examples. We both came from divorced homes and had our portion of childhood trauma. There were many nights that I asked, "Why am I doing this?" When I decided to have Tyler, I couldn't foresee the bumps in the road ahead. I guess that's why my dad was trying to protect me. At the time, a baby represented a new beginning for me. I thought a baby would wipe away my tears, bring better days, and lessen my pain. In the end, building a life with Xavier was an oxymoron of blessings and hardships.

"THE MOST OBVIOUS RED FLAG IS CALLED INTUITION..."

– Noel Maye

Chapter 9

Oh, No He Didn't

The most obvious red flag is called intuition.
—Noel Maye

X was a guy's guy, a ladies' man. Everyone loved his funny and charming personality. As for me? I loved his potential. I loved the idea of him, but not the real-time version of him. The possibility of loving this future X led me on a wild goose chase that had me waiting indefinitely for this person to show up. Now, don't get me wrong: there was a good guy stashed away in there who would peek out from time to time. It was *that* guy who kept me coming back for more. It was *that* guy who kept me constantly laughing until I almost peed myself on numerous occasions. Consequently, the laughter distracted us from the reality that we were two young kids trying to be functional adults. We were constantly running into emotional brick walls and having a battle of the egos. But the hope was to someday get this right, and that very hope kept me riding the emotional X roller coaster.

One beautiful afternoon in 2003, I had the day off from my job at Wells Fargo Bank. I'd snagged a full-time position as a personal banker after graduating college. It wasn't my dream job, but it paid the bills and offered flexibility so that I could pursue my childhood love of acting. I spend most of the day tidying up our second-story apartment in Rancho, San Diego, a suburb outside of Skyline. Our working-class neighborhood was a step up from the streets that we grew up in, and it was a safe place to raise our daughter. Today, Xavier was out with friends attending a cookout, and Tyler was spending the day with Naomi.

I took this time off to finally hang the piles of clean clothes that X had left lying on our bedroom floor for weeks. As I was emptying out the pockets of the countless pairs of X's Levi jeans so that I could toss them in the washing machine, lo and behold, a wrapped condom fell onto the floor.

"What in the hell?" I angrily stated aloud. "This fool is out of his mind!"

Pissed and shocked, I continued to read the receipts in his pockets in an attempt to connect the dots. In complete reaction mode, I called his cell phone to confront him about the condoms.

X answered his phone. "What's up, Brook?"

Without hesitation, I jumped down his throat. It was probably not the best approach. "I should be asking *you* that question," I replied.

"Oh, shit. What did I do now?" We had gone down this road before, and these types of questions weren't new to X.

I trembled on the other end of the phone and collected my thoughts.

"What the fuck is it, Brooklen? You are always comin' at me with this bullshit!" he exclaimed.

"I find it quite suspicious that you would jump down my throat without knowing the reason for my call, so let me get straight to the point. Why did I find a condom in the pocket of your Levi's?" I chose to mention the specific brand of jeans in hopes that it would help him remember when he'd committed his offense. I should've let his ass stumble and answer on his own.

"Really, Brooklen? Really? You are interrupting a perfectly good day to ask me about some damn condoms? See what *you* do?" he blamed me. "You ruin things when they are good." He always found a way to turn things around on me.

"Why are you always doing this? Why do you try to flip the script instead of answering the damn question? You know what? I don't need you to answer. I know what the hell I saw! So, fuck you, X. Don't bring your ass home!" I closed my phone and slammed it on the oak dresser given to me by M&M.

Filled with rage, I commenced to do the ungodly. I snatched up one shoe from every pair of Michael Jordan Nikes he owned, dropped them in a large black trash bag, and tossed them into the dumpster of our apartment complex. I threw away about a half dozen pairs of his precious Jordan cargo. All the while, I knew that would send him off the deep end. I couldn't care less. Just like he couldn't care less when he put his penis inside another woman.

A few hours later, the sun hid behind the mountains, and X arrived at our apartment. We wasted no time arguing about the slip in his character.

"So you are going to put our family through this shit again, X?" I stated as he walked down the hallway to our bedroom. I followed him. "Are you going to just play dumb and ignore me?"

"Brooklen, I don't have time for this. I don't care what you think you saw, and you can think what you want because I know the truth."

"Wow. So, you are going to act like I didn't find an unexpired, recently purchased condom in your jeans? So you were holding someone else's condom, Xavier? What do you think I am? An idiot?" I aggressively questioned him. My strategy sure wasn't working.

Damn. I'd set myself up with that question. My strategy was not working. He condescendingly replied, "Yup. It was someone else's."

In a completely frustrated attempt, I lunged from my bed to Xavier's back and repeatedly punched him all over his upper body and face. His lack of ownership in this situation fueled my raging fire. He continued to deny it, and I continued to spit verbal venom at him in an attempt to hurt him the way he'd hurt me.

"Fuck you, X! I hate you! I hope she was worth it! Matter of fact, have that whore buy you some new Jordans, because you need them now!" I shouted. I'd originally wanted him to find out what I had done on his own. My anger got the best of me as I watched X march down the hall in a frenzy to get to our closet and check on his babies.

"Brooklen!" he shouted after discovering that only one shoe of every pair was remaining on his side of the closet.

He came charging back down our hallway to the living room, where I stood anticipating what he'd do to me. Without hesitation, X picked me up in my low-cut tank top and panties, tossed me over his shoulder, and opened the front door to drop my petite body on the front porch. Then he slammed the door on me.

I stood there, embarrassed and in the cold. "Are you crazy? Open this damn door before someone sees me!"

"Open this door" was repeated for the next hour as X punished me for tossing his shoes in the trash. He punished me for reacting to *his* infidelity. How twisted was that? After what seemed like eternal banging on the door and pleading to get let back into the house for fear that someone would see me in my underwear, X finally untwisted the lock, but he left the door closed. He didn't even have the decency to open the damn thing. I walked in, and he retreated to the bedroom with the smell of cigarette smoke trailing behind him.

This display of anger was reminiscent of many instances in our past that caused me question whether this was true love. His fits of rage, his prolonged silent treatment, and my lack of verbal expression became the norm in our household. The good times were always met with equal (or worse) low times. After this bout with infidelity, I knew things weren't healthy, but I continued to stay in hopes that my love for him would triumph over these seemingly temporary battles. I had so much faith that we could weather these storms, and I was willing to be patient. My dream to not repeat my parent's broken home cycle was costing me big-time. The desire of "happily ever after" was more important to me than the truth. With that being said, just a few months later, I became his bride.

"DESTINY IS A NAME OFTEN GIVEN IN RETROSPECT TO CHOICES THAT HAD DRAMATIC CONSEQUENCES

JK Rowling

Chapter 10

Wedding Crashers

Destiny is a name often given in retrospect to
choices that had dramatic consequences.
—J. K. Rowling

About six months after Xavier's infidelity, I shoved my negative emotions under the rug and asked him what he thought about marrying me. I thought marriage would fix it. His lackluster response was enough for me to jump on the idea of planning the wedding. Up until this point, I had earned a college degree, and Tyler was growing up beautifully; we were essentially playing house. The most obvious next step was to get hitched and carry all this baggage into a lifelong commitment, right? I kept waiting for Xavier to outwardly profess his love for me and step up to the plate. After all, I believed I was a good catch, and I needed to help him see that. If he wasn't going to ask, then I was going to continue to probe.

One Saturday afternoon in the spring of 2004, we decided to go engagement ring shopping at Plaza Bonita Mall, just a few miles from our apartment. We hopped in our 2003 Toyota Camry and rode out to some Isley Brothers, Sisters with Voices, and Babyface. X always had a bangin' playlist; good music was one of the rare things that brought us together. He sang, and I listened and bobbed my head. I never felt comfortable singing around him for fear of judgment or criticism. That's how shattered and voiceless I had become—and yet I was guiding this ship right down a path to the altar.

"What are you thinking about?" I asked.

"Huh? Nothing. Why?"

"You always seem like there's something on your mind." I set Xavier up for a very common yet insecure question. "Do you think you'll be able to not cheat on me?"

"What? See, there you go. You always find a way to ruin everything!"

"Why do you get defensive instead of answering the question?" I always asked him this question. His answers never changed. Painful silence continued in the car for the next ten minutes. I was being punished for my question.

We arrived to the packed mall. Xavier's silence had at least turned into small talk, and so I didn't have to walk through the mall with a grown child. A couple of jewelry stores later, I settled on a massive princess-cut rose-gold engagement ring. The massiveness of the ring easily masked my diminished emotions. Many women excitedly waited for this day, and I was doing it in vain.

"You know, when a man buys a woman a rose-gold engagement ring, the couple stays married forever," said the woman behind the jewelry counter. X snickered, but that was sweet music to my soured heart.

After the no-brainer decision on my ring, we headed back home. Xavier was back in line emotionally and found our next jam to listen to. I sat in the passenger seat trading glances between the cars passing out the window and my new ring. Every good moment that we shared felt like the short-lived thrill from recreational drug use. The good was too far and in between for any healthy person, but for me, that little good kept me going.

We settled in at home on our comfy leather sectional and turned on the TV. *Martin* was on.

"So, Brook, you know I want to marry you, right?"

Without hesitation I responded, "Duh—you just bought me that fat ring!"

"Put it on, then," he commanded.

"I'm confused. Is this your proposal?"

"Yeah, why not? We already have a child together, and we love each other, right? Plus I ain't into all the fluffy stuff. I love you, so just put it on."

I listened. I slid the ring on my finger before he could change his mind.

It was no surprise that I didn't receive a dream proposal. I was settling—again. After all we had been through, the least I could get was a proper proposal. I sat on the couch with my gut twisted, wishing that I would have demanded something different.

Three short weeks later, we invited our immediate family members to the historic Old Town Park near downtown San Diego. This area was full of rich San Diegan culture, shops, and tourists from all over the world. The beautiful outside world was doing a good job of convincing me that I was feeling good about my inside world with X. Sadly, I decided not to invite all my family, because quite honestly I was embarrassed. I was lying to myself about doing the right thing in the wrong situation. Our friends and family were all rooting for us, and their happiness superseded my own.

"When are you guys getting married?"

"You are totally made for each other."

"You already have a child and live together. You may as well get married and stop shacking up!"

All these influences from loved ones pushed me to make choices based on their desires. I didn't feel that I had a voice, and I was drowning in their expectations. I was drowning in my own false expectations.

It was May 10, 2004, and we were about to take the plunge. I had been second-guessing my decision all day long, but I was too afraid to speak my truth. I didn't know how. In a perfect scenario, I'd have a beaming smile from here to the moon, gazing into the eyes of the man of my dreams. Instead, I felt myself being sucked into a vacuum that would continually toss me into a life of insecurity and what felt like insanity at times. The blissful fairy tale was feeling more like teeth being pulled while everyone I loved watched me silently suffer.

"Do you, Xavier, take Brooklen to be your lawful wedded wife? If so, say, 'I do,'" stated Pastor Dexter, a gentleman in his early seventies who towered over us with a presence that made me even more squeamish.

"I do," X responded.

"Do you, Brooklen, take Xavier to be your lawful wedded husband? If so, say, 'I do.'"

The knot in my throat was the size of a golf ball. I swallowed and stuttered my reply. "I d-d-do."

Cali stood behind me as my maid of honor. She wiped the beaded sweat off the back of my neck. I stood staring off in the distance to avoid making eye contact with Xavier. Rampant doubt clouded my mind as Xavier and I held sweaty palms. Our princess, Tyler, now four, stood next to me in her ivory-colored flower girl ensemble. Our family looked on proudly as we high school sweethearts were finally tying the knot. Their faces motivated me to carry on despite my fear.

"You may now kiss the bride," stated Pastor Dexter in his rich baritone that rivaled thunder itself.

The meeting of our lips was faster than the strike of a snake, and the ceremony was over. The crowd cheered, and I felt immediate relief. The air was released from my mental tire. Now it was time to get drunk. Xavier and I gathered into a black stretch Hummer limousine with eight of the craziest partygoers in our families. We cruised along the coastline with the sunroof opened, sipped Hennessy on the rocks, and smoked marijuana while we listened to Tupac, Anita Baker, and everything in between. The party was getting started!

X and I guzzled down several cups of liquor filled to the brim to numb the shock of what we had just done. Through it all, we'd made it down that altar to give our love a chance to make it right. We both glanced at each other in the back of the limo and declared in unison, "We did it."

Our coastline drive eventually led us to our dinner cruise reception near the San Diego airport. The limousine pulled up to the boat dock, where we prepared to embark on a classy excursion with dinner and dancing. The ladies and I hopped out of the Hummer and stumbled into the restroom, intoxicated, to take tinkles and air out our pretty dresses.

"I think I'm about to pee myself," I nervously shared.

"We're almost to the bathroom, Br—" Cali was frantically interrupted by Leo, my first cousin on Carol's side of the family. He was panicked.

"Brooklen, you guys need to get out here! X and his friends are fighting some guys in the middle of the street!" Sheer terror covered his face as he had to tell me about the ignorance taking place on my wedding day.

"What in the hell?" I slurred.

All the ladies began gathering their purses to hurry out.

"Follow me!" Leo demanded.

Leo led our small group of cousins and aunts out of the bathroom to see what was taking place in the middle of the street of the upscale community.

This was a nightmare. I stumbled to the edge of Pacific Highway to see Xavier atop of some big, burly white guy pounding his face into the concrete.

"X!" I screamed. "What in the hell are you doing? This is *my* wedding day!" I shouted in the hopes that the sound of my voice would cease his out-of-control behavior.

X continued to exchange punches in his tuxedo while his friends participated in about five other brawls all across the busy intersection. Complete mayhem took over my wedding day.

"Xavier, come on—stop it!" shouted Cali. "You have my sister in tears. Let's go!" she said as the police sirens were heard from down the block and the intensity of the moment increased.

Finally, X released his victim—but not before kicking him in the ribs one more time as he lay on the sidewalk just feet away from the dinner cruise entrance.

"I can't fucking believe you! It's our wedding day, X!" I shouted.

With guilt overtaking his entire demeanor, he apologized. "Brooklen, I know, I know. I'm so sorry! Damn. These fools started calling us names, and we had to show th—"

"Shut up. Just shut the hell up!" I demanded. "Hold my hand. The cops are coming, and you need to look like a civilized newlywed right now before you end up in jail."

Xavier and I paced quickly to board the cruise. I glanced across the street to the parking lot and saw our parents and extended family members also arriving.

"Oh my goodness. Here comes my father. Let's not say anything about this shit. This is so embarrassing."

"I get it, Brook. It's all good. Just chill," X suggested.

"Chill? Are you kidding me? You were just beating some man into a bloody pulp in public on our wedding day because he called you a name!" I ranted. "And those belligerent friends of yours are *not* getting on this boat. Now, let's move on. We have a reception to attend." At least I'd confidently expressed my disdain toward X. I mean, this was absolutely ridiculous.

One by one, approximately twenty of our wedding guests eagerly boarded the cruise ship. As I carefully walked up the staircase, I looked back to see five policemen arresting X's friends as several eyewitnesses told what they saw. The rest of us kept straight faces as if we hadn't just watched bodies flying in the air and punches swinging uncontrollably at the mercy of X and his crew. The poor gentlemen who X had beaten sat in the middle of the street, bloodied, while giving his testimony to the police. I continued onto the boat in full-on prayer that no one would identify my new husband. Xavier trailed closely behind me, looking sorrowful and downright embarrassed.

"You owe me one," I whispered back at Xavier with full intention to get my payment.

Once we made it to our seats for dinner on the Infinity Dream Cruise, we managed to enjoy the four-course meal that included fresh glazed Atlantic salmon, roasted garlic potatoes, seasonal spring vegetables, and freshly baked sourdough bread. Our dramatic day concluded with dancing to our favorite oldies and hits from the 2000s, eating lemon-infused wedding cake, and listening to words of support our loved ones. Throughout the night, my mind drifted, remembering moments from the brawl. I was relieved that our parents hadn't witnessed that foolishness. I could hear my father's voice telling me how he'd told me so.

No doubt this day would be one to remember, and it was a scary prophecy of the tone of our new marriage. One thing I learned was you can't mix alcohol and niggas. I loathe that word, but in this case, it applied.

"I DID IT THE STUPID WAY, THROUGH TRIAL AND ERROR."

— Jake Roberts

Chapter 11

I Don't

I did it the stupid way, through trial and error.
—Jake Roberts

I hated to admit it, but our wedding day was a huge sign of the danger that lay ahead. My spirit warned me, but my wants outweighed any truth that attempted to reach me. A few months into the marriage, neither of our needs were being met. We didn't fully understand the concept of giving selflessly in holy matrimony. I'd verbalized our wedding vows, but that was about it.

Shortly after our botched wedding day, I began actively pursuing my acting career, and I left him to hold down the "real job" so that I could make my dreams come true. I believed that I would become successful and eventually be able to take care of our family, allowing him to retire from the military early. There was a method to my madness, but he never truly supported my plan. I invested money, which he hated, and I put in the time to hone my craft. Month after month, I would attend auditions in the hopes of landing that magical gig that would shut him up and make us rich. There were countless road trips for mediocre work, and there were even local gigs that I believed took me one step closer. I was willing to sacrifice for my dream, but I didn't realize that the sacrifice was killing any remnants of what we called a marriage.

My lack of a financial contribution to our household affected my husband's feelings toward me and our relationship. Financially, he shared with

70

me that he felt alone, like the weight of the world was on his shoulders. The tension affected our intimacy and our daily interaction. Unfortunately, my entrepreneurial spirit was clashing with his safe nine-to-five mind-set. I wanted to dream, and he wanted me to earn a corporate check. Our relationship continued down this path of despair for the next few years until I couldn't take it anymore. I held on for my daughter. I held on for my family legacy. Lord knows that I didn't want to raise my daughter alone, but my hope was dimming.

"Cali, come over now. I need to get out of here!" I shouted after discovering a ripped piece of paper with a woman's phone number in Xavier's wallet.

"Okay, okay. Calm down, Brook. Tell me what happened," Cali replied.

"It doesn't matter anymore. Nothing matters anymore. Like I told you before, X can't control himself. I found another number in his wallet. I can't believe this shit," I disappointedly stated.

"Brook, breathe. Give me a minute. I'm hopping in the truck, and I'm on my way." Cali prepared to hang up.

"Hey, before you go, can you bring a couple of boxes?" I slowed down to ask for what I needed. "I'm not playing. I've really gotta go." Tears welled in my eyes.

Cali arrived at our apartment about half an hour after our phone conversation. I immediately began loading up the belongings that I could fit into her never-dirty ghost-white F-150 truck. Cali was such a kick-ass chick with her tinted windows and deafening stereo system. She always had my front, back, and all around. When no one else was there, Cali was there. Our unpredictable childhood led us to be consistent staples in each other's lives. Cali's loyalty was just like her: golden.

Meanwhile, Xavier had no clue this was happening. The military flew him to Texas on business for the week, which was perfect for my plot. My sole purpose of leaving while he was gone was to create shock value beyond this world when he returned home. I wanted him to feel what I felt. I wanted our empty apartment to serve as a major blow to his gut, just like every woman's phone number that I discovered. I packed up just about everything except one TV and his clothes. Did I feel bad at all? A little, but that didn't stop me.

"Okay, sissy, you are all packed up." Cali walked closer to me and placed her hand on my shoulder. "You really did it."

I stood in the doorway, looking into my near-empty apartment. "Yeah, I did." I paused. "And I hope this shit hits him like a Mac truck."

The anger brewed inside me as I recounted betrayal after betrayal. I felt unsupported, unloved, and ignored by Xavier. I wasn't being physically abused, but I felt the pain of his wrath emotionally. Our bouts led to his silent treatment and passive-aggressive behavior, which always left me feeling defeated. I tried to constantly prove my love to X, and I became exhausted and unsatisfied in the process. I worked so hard to fill his voids, but I failed to realize my own emotional bank was in the red. I was like a rabbit chasing a carrot dangling just low enough for me to taste it with the tip of my tongue, but never close enough to actually possess it. On this day, I left all my pain on that apartment floor without any clue of what the future held.

'EVEN THOUGH YOU'RE FED UP, YOU GOTTA KEEP YOUR HEAD UP."

- Tupac Shakur

Chapter 12

His Love; My Pain

Even though you're fed up, you got to keep your head up.
—Tupac Shakur

Immediately after moving out, I was living on pins and needles, anticipating a violent reaction from Xavier. Approximately two weeks had gone by, and I hadn't see him. One afternoon in early 2005, I was driving down Paradise Valley Road, parallel to the center of Skyline Drive, after picking up Tyler from preschool. As I was chatting with Tyler about her day, I glanced to my left and saw X at a gas station near our old apartment. We briefly made eye contact, and I saw that demon in his eyes. I was not going to be his victim that day, especially because we'd had no communication since prior to his business trip. I could only imagine his buildup. On the other hand, it was difficult keeping Tyler away from him, but I did what I felt was best for the both of us. A month without her dad would not be the end of the world. Well, I hoped not.

Now that I was living back at home with my mother, I found that some unresolved issues between she and I quickly resurfaced. Admittedly, our relationship was volatile due to her past addiction, but we always had a kindred place in our hearts for one another. I guess the fact that our birthdays were only days apart had something to do with our ambiguous relationship. We shared mannerisms and nuances in our speaking voices, but we felt divided in our characters. Throughout my childhood, her emotionally manipulative habits created in me a codependency issue that I struggled to conquer.

"Mom, when you get a chance, I really want to talk to you." I checked in with my mom while at our two-story townhome in the middle-class suburb of Paradise Hills.

"Okay, well, I've had a really long day. Will this be a good talk or a bad talk?"

This was my mother's way of feeling out the content of the conversation. If it was going to be anything that would threaten her ego or make her feel like the bad guy, then she would find a way to avoid it or cry her way out of it.

"Well, I wanted to respond to your question the other day about putting your new car in my name. I don't think it's a good id—"

I became distracted by Carol softly sobbing in the next room. I stopped cutting up the onion and green bell pepper that I was preparing for our chicken enchilada dinner. I needed a closer listen to what I thought I was hearing.

"Mom, are you crying in there?"

She abruptly responded, "Just forget it. Forget it! No one is ever there when I need them. I'll take care of it," she pouted.

I was familiar with Carol using crying or guilt-tripping tactics toward me and others to get what she wanted. I was being tricked again. I walked into the room she was occupying. "What do you mean? Cali and I are always there for you. In fact, we are the only people you can depend on! Why do you do this?"

I stood there, stinky onion hands and all, with the purest look of bafflement. Had she mastered making me feel guilty for sharing my honest feelings? Yup, she'd won again. I signed the loan papers later that day and increased my debt in order to make her happy. But where was my happiness in the equation? Oh, yeah—my happiness wasn't ever considered.

My unhealthy belief was that constant sacrifice and pain were necessary to have successful relationships. I never wanted to hurt anyone's feelings, and those behaviors that I learned at home, interacting with my parents, eventually played out with Xavier. I realized that moving back with my mother perpetuated this manipulative, codependent dynamic. My mom and X would use their selfish ways to play mind games in order to get what they felt they needed. X would use things like silent treatment to control our relationship; my mom would be overly dramatic, cry, and use guilt trips to keep me at bay. On the surface, moving back home was a positive choice, but it certainly kept me in an emotional place that I was trying to escape. Ironically, my mom was selfish in many ways, but there wasn't anything that she wouldn't do for her children. I knew without a shadow of a doubt that come hell or high water, she would be there when I needed her most. I guess that's why I kept being sucked into her web.

Contrarily, my other experience of being mothered came from Xavier's mom, Naomi. Naomi was a strong-minded, college-educated, professional woman. She held her ground in her Christian beliefs and had raised three boys all on her own. She was one of my top supporters throughout college, encouraged my dreams, and wanted the best for me as a fellow mother and woman. I spent a lot of time between my mom's house and hers, especially because she was such a big help with Tyler. We were so close that it made some folks uncomfortable, including Xavier. He didn't like it very much that I continued to spend time with Naomi even though he and I weren't together anymore. My relationship with her was healthy and strong, and it was a shame that I couldn't say the same for my marriage to her son.

One Sunday afternoon, my daughter and I went over to Naomi's house to help work on her new vegetable garden. Before we headed out into the backyard to dig holes and plant seeds, I wanted to make sure we were properly using our little green thumbs. I hopped on the internet in Naomi's bedroom and kept the door open so that I could keep an eye on Tyler playing in the living room. I began searching for planting techniques for our new veggie project, and then I heard a voice come from the front door greeting Tyler. It was none other than X. He'd popped up to shower Tyler with his grandiose display of affection, while making it obvious he was ignoring me. The spite filled the house so quickly, and the sharpest of knives couldn't have cut it. I got it: he was still pissed at the way I'd moved out of our apartment.

"Yeah, man. I will come through the spot after I visit my son," Xavier boldly said to the person he was talking to on the phone.

Uh, what did I just hear this fool say? Did he just say "my son"?

76

Did the man who I am still married to just say that he needed to go see his son? Okay, I could have heard that incorrectly. Let me calm my nerves and act like I'm still searching for these gardening techniques. However, my heart was in my stomach and I was sweating bullets. Xavier stayed on the phone for a few more minutes before he left the house. I didn't say anything to him at the moment. Once the door closed behind him, I immediately walked out to the front porch, where Naomi was smoking a cigarette.

Without hesitation I asked, "Did I hear him correctly? Did he say that he had a son?"

Naomi looked at me disappointedly and said, "Yes. He just found out a few days ago, but I don't have any details. I'm sorry you had to find out that way, honey."

I jumped right in to respond. "Well, whose is it? I mean, what? Is he sure?" I asked in a state of complete shock.

"Apparently, the DNA test came back 99 percent positive, proving that he was the father of the boy," she stated. "So, yes, he's sure."

I sobbed due to my feelings of complete betrayal. The statistics that I was so adamantly running from were chasing me down. A child outside of our marriage? Damn. I'd never thought that would be me. But never say never.

"He said it was some one-night stand. The child is almost one," she added.

"One? Where the hell has he been hiding this whole time! I cannot believe this shit."

"It sounded like the girl was scared to tell him, because he got pretty aggressive with her over the phone. She kept the baby a secret until recently," she dished.

I appreciated her input considering the fact that Xavier had neglected to give his wife any explanation. Thank goodness Naomi was there to help me connect the pieces.

"He wanted to know the truth, and so he agreed to take a test. It was obvious to me that the results were not what he was wishing for."

"No shit," I quickly replied. "I'm pretty sure having a baby with trailer-park trash while being married with a family was not on his bucket list." My sarcasm served as a rug pulled over my shattered heart.

"I know, sweetie." Naomi moved across the front porch to grab my hand. "We never hope to deal with circumstances like this. But, honey, this isn't your fault. X made his bed, and now he has to lie in it."

My heartbeat pounded inside my ears as I poured my tears onto the porch. Despite the betrayal and gut-wrenching pain I felt, all I could think about was Tyler and how this situation would affect her life. What a selfish asshole, to risk permanently losing his family for one night of sex. Out of all his infidelities, this one hit me the hardest. Not only did he have a child with someone else, but she'd given him a male child. The bitch had given *my* husband a son.

Over the next few grieved months, I asked God why he would allow something like this to happen. Why did this have to be my situation? I worked so hard to live a drama-free life, but here I was in a Maury Povich situation. Of course, this was not my fault, but the pain of the consequences seemed to fall on me. The agony of imagining all the different scenarios that may have taken place between my husband and this woman was like walking on hot coals. I tried to justify how something like this could happen in order to lessen the blow, but it didn't work.

One day while driving into work, I was praying. All of a sudden, I started yelling at God in anger. "How could you let this happen? Why me? How could another woman give to my husband the thing that I was supposed to give him?"

I was so embarrassed, and I hadn't even done anything. God was on my list of not-so-caring people. Although I believed that everything happened for a reason, I still couldn't deny the pain that I felt. At the same time that I was upset with God, I had to put my trust in him for the answers. I trusted that though this was a crappy situation, I would come out okay on the other end.

I obsessed about my husband's infidelity and outside child for months to come. I wanted to know everything about this woman. I needed to know who this woman was and why he thought it was worth losing everything all for her. Did she look better than me? Was she smart? Did she work with him? Did I know her? My investigation ensued until one Saturday afternoon in early 2006.

I stopped by Naomi's to pick up my mail per usual. Unbeknownst to me, there were some visiting arrangements made with the skank and her illegitimate child stopping by Naomi's. I felt bad calling him that, but based on the situation, that was exactly what he was: a bastard. I understood that Naomi wanted to at least attempt to build a relationship with the boy, and I wasn't going to let that happen without Tyler and me a part of it. Tyler had been the only grandchild, and I had strong feelings about this kid coming in to steal the shine. We hung around in the living room so we could meet these people.

"Tyler, you know how Mommy said that Daddy has a baby, and he's your little brother?" I couldn't figure out how to have this conversation. "Well, he is coming by to say hello with his mommy."

Tyler stared out of the window expressionless. There was no easy way to explain to a six-year-old that she had a new sibling that only days prior she had no idea existed.

Within moments, Xavier's son, Cameron, and his mother, Jennifer, were pulling up in front of Naomi's home. Tyler and I watched from the living room as she unloaded the baby from the car. They began their trod up the driveway, and I locked eyes with the one-year-old. Immediately I felt a connection with him. I couldn't figure out where this was coming from, but it took over my anticipated rage. I had compassion for the child. I looked at his pale skin, sandy blond kinky hair, and his most prominent feature, my husband's trademark eyes. Tyler had the same eyes. And because he was biologically a part of my husband, I felt that he was a part of me too.

Jennifer was an average-looking blonde who carried an "out of town" vibe. I could tell that she wasn't from San Diego because of her laid-back outfit and hiking boots. Considering the fact that they'd met at work, there was a high probability that she was from the Midwest. Nonetheless, her looks confirmed that whatever they shared was driven by pure lust and a few bottles of alcohol.

She dropped Cameron off at Naomi's to return later. The child gravitated toward me, and I showed him love. After all, what his two stupid parents did had nothing to do with him. He was innocent. Considering the fact that he was biracial, I thought I would help his mother out and braid his hair. It was heavily mangled and dry, which indicated to me that she didn't know what the hell she was doing.

The visit was quite short, and Jennifer returned about an hour later. Tyler played with Cameron on the living room rug and read books to him as I combed his hair. Naomi watched from a distance and periodically came in to engage. I believed that Jennifer was trying to connect Naomi to Cameron in the hopes that he would know the other side of his family. Cameron's short visit was a first step toward initiating that relationship.

"Mommy, it looks like my brother's mommy is back. I see a red car pulling up," shared Tyler as she peeked out of the living room window.

I gathered my husband's son's toys and clothing while Naomi finished cleaning his bottles in the kitchen. "Okay, sweetie. Thank you," I nervously replied.

I was getting ready to face this woman again, and I'd extended myself to comb her son's hair, which could have crossed a line.

"Come on in, Jennifer," Naomi shouted from the kitchen. I sat on the living room sofa with her son on my lap.

A part of me felt like I was winning. Her son loved me, and I was still present in my husband and his family's life, which meant there was no room for her. I was the leading lady in Xavier's life, regardless of our situation. At least, that was how I felt.

"Um, hi, Naomi. What did you do to Cameron's hair?" she asked.

"Oh, yes. Brooklen wanted to help out and put a few braids in his hair. You like them?"

I sat there with an internal smirk, hoping this broad said something about it. Instead, with a look of pure shock and disgust, Jennifer grabbed her from my lap along with his belongings. She began to move toward the front door. "I would have appreciated if someone would have called to ask me," she stated as my jaws dropped at the fact that she'd spoken to either of us in that tone. "I know that I don't know you all very well, but I'm just not used to this." She fixed that tone really quick. *Girl, please.*

She firmly expressed her feelings to Naomi and shuffled out the front door with nothing more than a goodbye. I guessed seeing those tiny ponytails covering her precious child's head threw her for a loop. Once she drove off, I laughed at her response to his hair, but simultaneously I cried on the inside that this woman had my husband. I was getting some pleasure out of her frustration, but I still felt unsatisfied.

Naomi and X had a few more visits with Cameron before his mother moved him out of state. According to X, like many women she believed that having a baby could keep him near or even get him to commit. The irony was that X barely knew her last name, but she wanted to try to keep him? She thought she would take a man away from his family? I couldn't lie: when they left San Diego, I felt a sigh of relief. Out of sight, out of mind.

"RATHER THAN
TURNING THE PAGE,
IT'S MUCH EASIER TO
JUST THROW THE
BOOK AWAY."

— Anthony Liccione

Chapter 13

Change Your Thoughts, Change Your Life

Rather than turning the page, it's much easier
to just throw the book away.
—Anthony Liccione

After months of struggling to make the end of our marriage official, I decided to file for a divorce in the spring of 2005. Honestly, after Jennifer, I had accepted enough, and there was reasonable cause to simply walk away. As much as my broken heart wanted to stay, the logical side of me said that I deserved more. Our divorce was pretty simple considering that we didn't have any assets and only our daughter to share. I knew that X wouldn't give me any issues with Tyler because he didn't want the full responsibility of raising a child anyway. It would be right up his alley to visit her and give money. That way, he would still have the freedom to do what he wanted, when he wanted, and with whom he wanted.

Before I knew it, I was a twenty-five-year-old divorced mom ready to find myself. This new freedom gave me the opportunity to try things that I always wanted but felt that I couldn't. I did more acting in television and commercials, and I modeled as well. I landed my biggest gig yet as a tennis shoe model in *Vibe Magazine*. During the summer of 2005, I remained roommates with my mother, and we took advantage of an opportunity to purchase our first home together with Cali. It was a three-bedroom fixer-upper east of our Skyline neighborhood. Unfortunately, this part of town didn't lack gang activity, but we managed to stay safe. My life was progressing, and I was moving on from X. This seemed to have been the best decision I had ever made.

The sun perfectly warmed the day on my way home from Sunday service. I stopped to grab a bite at a small pizza joint in Paradise Hills, a couple of miles south of Skyline. I saw a nice-looking man in his early forties eyeballing me from the parking lot. I tilted my black shades down and peeked over the rim in order to discover whether or not I knew the man.

"Excuse me, miss. Have you seen this magazine? Our financial services company has been featured in it this month."

The gentleman was sharply dressed in a professional suit, stood about six feet tall, and was cleanly shaven and good smelling. He handed me a business magazine titled *Success*. The glossy cover and bold, powerful print caught my attention.

"No, I don't think I have seen this before," I replied.

He walked closer toward me. "Well, are you allergic to making extra income?"

My eyes widened. "Allergic?" I laughed right in this gentleman's face. "Absolutely not."

We exchanged phone numbers, and this single transaction would open a door that would forever change my life.

I was searching for a way to live out my dreams, and this could be it for me. This could be the light at the end of the tunnel that I'd desperately yearned for since divorcing Xavier. A perfect stranger introduced me to the entrepreneurial world, and I was ready. *Success* shared story after story of everyday folks just like me living extraordinary lives. I saw an alternative to the nine-to-five grind that I so desperately loathed, and for the first time in my working life, I saw an opportunity to provide for my daughter and a place to fit in. I always felt in my heart that I was going to find a way to make lots of money. I believed I had found my financial savior.

Becoming an entrepreneur not only introduced me to new ways of thinking and making money, but it expanded my wish list for the type of man I wanted. There was one particular gentleman, Devin James, who was an extremely successful financial planner with the company. In fact, he was a millionaire. Devin was a true rags-to-riches story with the charisma to match. His slightly muscular build could sport a three-piece suit any day of the week, not to mention his sparkling green eyes drew in every onlooker. He was absolutely dreamy. When I first saw him in that magazine, I told myself that we would meet one day. I didn't know how or when, but I knew without a shadow of a doubt that he would have the pleasure of meeting little ol' me.

Just a few months into my new venture, I busted my butt in the financial planning sales division, and as a result I earned tens of thousands of dollars in bonuses and free vacations. Things were looking up for Brooklen Sapphire. The very first vacation I won was to the breathtaking landscapes of Lake Tahoe, which was about a twelve-hour drive away from home. I brought my mother as my guest, and we hopped on a plane and prepared ourselves for a weekend of relaxation.

Upon arrival to the quaint town, we were welcomed with a classy breakfast, coupled with some powerhouse speakers in the financial industry. To my surprise, one of the guest speakers was Devin James. Mr. James graced the stage as I stared in total shock. Perhaps I was bringing what I'd once thought about into my real life.

"Nothing great is achieved without first enduring …" Those were the closing remarks as Devin prepared to exit the stage in the small banquet hall. My mother and I clapped for what felt like eternity as I watched him powerfully descend from the stage. The whole scene replayed in my head when that stranger had handed me the magazine with Devin's story. Wow, would I really get the chance to meet him? My mom and I shuffled against the crowd out the door and up to our tenth-floor suite.

Ring, ring, ring …

I hesitated to answer the blocked phone number calling my cell. I wasn't really in the mood for business calls or telemarketers, but I decided to answer it anyway.

"Hello, is Brooklen Sapphire available?" The voice had an ounce of familiarity.

I reluctantly replied, "Yes. May I ask who's calling?"

"This is Devin James. You left your business cards in the breakfast room."

What? I just about fainted on the hotel room floor at hearing his voice on the other end. I jumped up and down, flailing my arms in an attempt to get my mom's attention as she stood on the terrace smoking a cigarette and talking on the phone. I mouthed to her who was on the phone with the excitement of a teen girl who'd been asked to the prom.

"Who?" I asked, attempting to gain my composure.

"It's Devin James. Would you like your business cards back?" he asked in a witty tone.

Of course I wanted them back, and I absolutely wanted to meet him. Devin and I made arrangements to get together in the lobby later on that evening. This had to be fate. Honestly, couldn't he have turned my cards into the front desk, or even more simple, left them in the banquet hall from earlier that morning? This man wanted to meet me, and little did he know that I had willed this day into existence months prior. Thoughts are things.

"Brooklen?" Devin inquired as he stood just a few feet away from me in the plush hotel lobby.

"Yes, Devin. I know that face," I joked. "Well, of course I know your face. You're all over magazines and stages everywhere. Um, let me shut up. Yes, I'm Brooklen. It's very nice to meet you." I embarrassingly responded to the man I had admired from afar for months. What a freaking mess, fumbling over my words. I talk too damn much. "I am assuming you wanted to give me my business cards back?"

Duh.

"I couldn't help but notice how beautiful you are, which is why I held onto them all day." He gave a sly grin, showing what seemed like an attraction toward me.

I blushed. "Thank you, Devin—Mr. James. Wait, should I just call you Devin?" There goes Fumbalina again.

"Devin is fine." He smiled some more, only that time I got to see those perfect ivories in his mouth. "Hey, I'm not sure if you are busy, but I was getting ready to take a break from the crowds and duck out to the beach. You wouldn't want to join me, would you?"

It took the life of me to keep my composure. "Sure, I'm free."

Devin and I made our way through the lobby to the Spanish-styled double doors at the Lake Tahoe Resort, and we were interrupted. Droves of admiring business associates awaited outside, hoping to catch a photo or even a quick word of inspiration from Devin. I stood in the background, waiting for the hype to die down. My arms were lightly crossed against the cleavage that peeked through my floral print maxi dress. My long hair flowed in unison with the winds blasting through the hotel doors.

"Thanks, guys, for the love and congrats on earning this amazing incentive trip," he encouraged the crowd. "Make sure you all make time to relax. That's exactly what I'm getting ready to do."

He looked over at me, and I smiled. We began our stroll to the beach. Our chance meeting was marked with great conversation, tons of laughs, and a mutual respect for our accomplishments. After all, we were both hard-working entrepreneurs enjoying the fruits of our labor on an amazing trip, and the cherry on top was meeting. We had mad respect for one another. Devin and I continued to fill our vacation weekend with late-night talks on the beach and flirtatious text messages. I didn't want the weekend to end, but we all know what happens to good things.

I lay in my hotel bed each night in awe of the sheer coincidence that out of the hundreds of people in attendance, Devin James had found *my* business cards. I was beginning to believe that what I desired and envisioned could truly come to fruition. I mean, that was exactly what was happening to me.

"Can I walk you to the shuttle? I really hate to see you go," Devin uttered to me outside of my hotel room door.

I hated that it was time to say goodbye. I was on such a high and didn't want to come down. Was this just a weekend fling? "Of course you can walk me down. I wouldn't have it any other way."

My departure was the pitiful reality that our whirlwind weekend had come to an end. The adrenaline from meeting Devin depleted as I slowly approached the shuttle. "Let's not make this our last time seeing each other," I ventured. "I enjoyed you—the jokes, the banter, the connection. It was a nice treat to have met you this weekend."

We embraced.

He said, "I felt that too. I have an upcoming trip to New York. Maybe you could find time to take another vacation?"

Well, that was music to my ears.

"Take care, and see you at the top, Brooklen." He laughed.

Devin couldn't help but give me a couple of entrepreneurial words of encouragement.

"You too."

I preferred that he kept it all mushy, so I digressed. I hung onto his words like the air that I breathed. Devin James was absolutely into me.

Our fast-paced romance lasted less than a year. We maximized our time together with extended weekend trips from the West Coast to the East Coast and everywhere in between. Our late-night conversations lit up with our favorite songs, our children, and our careers. The highlight would always be finding the next city to catch one of our favorite comedians.

We kept our love affair under wraps for a few reasons. I was a burgeoning leader in the company, and he was an established one. Neither one of us wanted to compromise what we were building, at least not this early on. I loved his mind and sense of humor. He was a flat-out quality man. But before things got a chance to deepen, we mutually agreed it wasn't a good time for something serious. I regretfully backed off Mr. Devin James because the truth was I still had some open wounds. I wasn't quite out of the emotional woods regarding Xavier, but Devin served as a beautifully timed distraction. We both respected each other, and I stayed focused on my hustle.

"LUST FEELS LIKE
LOVE UNTIL IT'S TIME
TO MAKE A SACRIFICE."

– Author Unknown

Chapter 14

Lessons in Love

Lust feels like love until it's time to make a sacrifice.
—unknown

Devin exited the front doors of my life, and before I could bat an eye, Kalvin reentered. Kalvin was a past flame I'd met shortly after I'd started my financial planning business. A mutual college friend introduced me to the disgustingly handsome, thought-provoking businessman. He drove nice cars, dressed well, and fluently spoke three languages. But Kalvin could also take it to the streets by any means necessary, and he smelled damn good doing it all. He was pretty much Mr. Perfect.

Kalvin and I had had some drama early on with a jealous ex-girlfriend, and I decided to graciously bow out of the affair. We also lived in two different cities, which made spontaneous five-hour drives pretty tough after a while. But there we were, finding ourselves back in each other's beds and making those midnight drives from one city to the next in the name of … love? Lust?

Kalvin challenged me mentally. This was something that I hadn't experienced in any relationship. I was used to carrying the relationship with Xavier and not having an equal to pick up some of the weight. He was twelve years my senior with a flourishing real estate company and adult children. This relationship caused me to step up my game, and I was up for the challenge.

In addition to mind-riveting conversations, we shared vagina-numbing sex. Our deep talks nearly always led us to the bedroom to share our deepest parts with one another. I mean, don't get me wrong: we liked each other's character. But the wiles of euphoric sex kept us endlessly coming back for more. We spent nearly half a year before our fling became the real thing.

"Cali, answer your damn phone," I uttered as her ringtone played classical elevator music that annoyed the crap out of me.

"Hello?" Cali answered right before I hung up.

"Hey, are you busy?"

"What is it, Brook? You never care if I'm busy."

"Well, so … shit," I stammered. "Um … My period is a few days late, and I don't want to jump to conclusions, but—"

"What? By who? I mean, I don't mean it like that. I'm not saying you're a ho or anything. But you know? Well, who is it?"

"Kalvin. The one where we had a thing about a year ago and then recently started again. The realtor," I embarrassingly replied.

"Oh, yeah, him. The one with the crazy-ass ex." Cali had jokes. "So, what now? Did you tell him?"

"No. Let me take a test, and then I can figure this shit out. Damn!" I shouted.

In less than twenty-four hours, I had bought pregnancy tests from 7-11, Walmart, and Ralph's Grocery Store. Without fail, each one said positive. I was in so much denial that I had to pee on multiple sticks in order to stomach the truth. I quickly called Carol and Cali to update them on my news. Now I had to tell the father of my child. The truth was we were only friends and lovers, but parents? We were nowhere near marriage. I mean, Kalvin was great, wonderful even, but to put my life on hold to have a child with someone I wasn't even sure would be in my life next year was fearsome.

I nestled in my bed under my Donna Karan comforter set while Tyler was at school. I flipped open my phone and called him. "Hey, Kalvin. I need to chat with you. Do you have a minute?"

"B, what's up? You sound nervous." Kalvin patiently waited for a response.

"I can't lie. I am super nervous," I affirmed. "Well, it's one thing to enjoy our time and have great sex together. There's no pressure in a relationship like that." I hoped to soften the shock. "But how would you feel about becoming a daddy again?"

The long, quiet pause on the other end of my phone was intense. "What are you saying, B? I know you're not pregnant. Are you?"

Kalvin's tone sounded like he hoped this news wasn't true. As I uttered the confirmation of my pregnancy, my heart sank, and I saw my future flash right before my eyes. What the heck would I tell Tyler? She was only seven years old and had no clue that I was dating men other than her daddy. I didn't want two kids, let alone by two different men. This was not how I'd envisioned my future at all. I was supposed to be traveling the country and growing a large business. A baby had no place in my new life.

One week later, Kalvin and I met for lunch about halfway between our residences in Los Angeles to further discuss our issue at hand. After the two-and-a-half-hour drive up, I parked in a Denny's parking lot and hopped into the passenger side of his black Lincoln Navigator SUV. After a few moments of painful silence, we began the conversation. For nearly an hour, Kalvin eloquently convinced me that an abortion was the best thing for us both, mainly focusing on the strain it would put on our growing careers. We were both practicing Christians, but in the blink of an eye, all our morals went out of the window. Kalvin successfully tipped the scales of my decision, and I scheduled the appointment. He paid for it, and I suffered for it.

"Lord, protect Brooklen as she goes into this procedure. Forgive her for her sins and remove her guilt. She loves you. Help her to never compromise her beliefs in the future. Lord, please heal her physically and spiritually. We seal this prayer in Jesus's name. Amen."

That was the prayer uttered between my two supportive yet opinionated best friends, Kasha and Jules, two sharp ladies from the business world. The two drove me to a small clinic in downtown San Diego, away from any opportunity to see someone I knew. On the drive down, I thought about how contradictory that prayer was, asking for forgiveness before I willingly committed another act against God. I felt selfish but continued along with the plan. After all, I didn't see myself being tied to Kalvin in this permanent way, and I knew he didn't really want this baby. It simply wasn't in the plan, and so I justified the abortion.

I lay on the table, alone and scared, as the doctor pulled the baby from my body. The guilt ripped apart my heart, and a tear fell from my eye and onto the cold surgery table. I felt like shit. I was a vessel of life that cursed my own blessing to death. Tyler would never meet her sibling, at least not in this lifetime.

Days after experiencing one of the most disgraceful moments in my adult life, I started to blame Kalvin for the decision I'd made. *If he loved me, then he would have wanted the baby. He convinced me it was the best thing to do, and I believed him. I wasn't good enough to be the mother of his child.* These were some of the guilt-driven thoughts that I repeatedly told myself—and even worse, I opened my mouth to share them with Kalvin. The termination of my pregnancy did something to me. It changed me, and I vowed to never put myself in a situation like that again. If I were to ever become pregnant in this lifetime, I was going to own up to my responsibility. If I would have just saved myself for marriage, then I wouldn't have had to worry about getting knocked up by some noncommittal man. When it came to Kalvin, my human desires always won over my moral compass.

Needless to say, the abortion took a toll on our relationship, and I couldn't look at him in the same way. I decided to move on without him, and unfortunately he took a piece of me with him. A permanent scar was made on my soul, and I continued to ask God for his forgiveness. The hard part was forgiving myself.

"WHAT'S MEANT TO BE
WILL ALWAYS FIND A
WAY."

—Trisha Yearwood

Chapter 15

Fate's Child

What's meant to be will always find a way.
—Trisha Yearwood

Nearly a year had gone by since the decision was made to terminate my pregnancy. I moved on by burying myself under work and making money. On the happier side of the summer of 2008, I was now a stable homeowner, with my mother and sister as investing partners. We were all independent women making our dreams happen. In the midst of such growth, there was underlying unhappiness. I struggled to bounce back after experiencing back-to-back traumas. I continued to want more out of life but kept succumbing to the weight of my emotional baggage.

A couple of years after my separation from Xavier, I noticed the lingering hope for our relationship. Even while I was living my life and seemingly happy, there was a part of me that felt I may have ended things too soon. Go figure—he still had a hold on me. The few relationships I had managed to end for one reason or another, and Xavier was familiarity. I'd known the guy since I was fifteen, and there was something about going back home. My gut told me to stay away and be strong, but I curiously wanted to see if there was any love left.

Skyline was shaken by another murder. Cliff Johnson, a high school football star and local celebrity, was gunned down at a nearby liquor store after a game. Cliff was also the younger cousin of Xavier. The neighborhood was shocked because Cliff had a clean reputation and aspirations of reaching the NFL. This young one had a bright future.

Meanwhile, I hadn't spoken to Xavier prior to his cousin's murder. We had a pretty no-nonsense visitation schedule for Tyler, which left minimal room for casual conversation. I wanted to pay my condolences.

"X?" I said as if I hadn't just picked up the phone and dialed his cell number.

"Yeah?" he dryly replied.

"I heard about Cliff. I'm so sorry. I know we haven't spoken much lately, but you know that I still care about you." I paused. "So, I wanted to check on you." I attempted to push on whatever door may still be open there. I was yearning to fill this nagging hole in my life, and strangely, I thought Xavier could still be the answer.

"Well, that is nice of you, but I don't need you checking on me. I'm good."

Xavier zapped any air that I had in my little balloon. I was trying to uplift, but he aimed to shut down.

"Wow. I get it. I was just trying to show some love," I protested.

"Brook, you didn't even like Cliff. Get out of here with that fake shit. Don't you have a business to run?"

I sat looking out of my kitchen window. My jaw dropped. "Damn, X. This is exactly why I keep my distance from you. You always want to go there, thinking that I'm out to get you. You know what? Your wish is my command. I'll see you around."

I hung up the phone, picked up my Hennessy and Coke from the kitchen counter, and charged to my bedroom. The nerve of him. A few short moments after I walked into my room, Xavier called back to apologize, and he asked if I would come over without Tyler. I fussed at him for about ten minutes before giving in. I quickly freshened up in the bathroom and slid on my Seven jeans, a SDSU hoodie, and red Uggs to match. I popped on some lip gloss, tossed my hair around a bit, and was out the door.

The rain cascaded down my windshield as I carefully shifted through the slippery streets. My thoughts of meeting Xavier overpowered the pounding raindrops. *What in the hell am I doing? Why did I decide to meet this man alone? Am I walking into a trap? Does he still want me?*

After a short three-mile drive, I arrived at Naomi's, where Xavier was currently staying. I hopped out of my silver Lexus ES300 smelling like the sweet scent of jasmine and honey mixed with Dove soap. Xavier awaited my arrival on the porch looking good as ever. His athletic build screamed, "Take me, Brooklen." I fought every urge to run up and kiss him. My perplexed feelings crept up as I approached the porch. I thought without a shadow of a doubt that I was done with this man. He'd put me through hell, but there I was, walking toward him with a glimmer of curiosity and hope in my eyes.

"So, what's up, X? Why did you want me to come over?"

Not only did he have a girlfriend, but he also had plans to move across the country with her in a month or so. To be quite frank, I had no concern for this girl because I believed that I was Xavier's one and only true love. Suddenly, my motive changed. To think he could potentially love someone else caused me to feel threatened, and I couldn't let that happen. Even though I was the one who'd left him, a piece of me still wanted to remain the sovereign ruler of his heart.

Within the first half hour of meeting, our conversation turned into passionate kissing and fondling. I knew that I could still have him, and I did just that.

"Stop. Just stop. What are we doing, Brooklen?" Xavier said as he slowly stopped penetrating my body on his mom's elegantly dressed guest bed.

"We are having sex. Why are you talking?" I responded, hoping to succeed at my plot to prove who the real queen was in his life.

I felt his emotions detaching with every thrust. He wanted out. "Wait, wait. I just can't do this."

"What the hell do you mean, you can't do this? I am butt naked, and you are having second thoughts?"

"This is wrong. We can't have these feelings for each other anymore."

He pulled his pants up and left me lying there like the end pieces of a loaf of bread.

"Oh, so all of a sudden you have a conscience? What the hell did you invite me over for? To talk? We could have done that shit over the phone!" I slid back on my clothes, grabbed my Dooney & Bourke bag, and stormed out of the front door with my shoes in hand. I knew this was a crazy idea. Why the hell did I think meeting my ex-husband was a good idea? He was still playing mind games, and I was still in his web. *Damn, Brooklen, you know better than this.* I proved that I could have him, but then he discarded me like yesterday's trending topic. In our marriage, I commonly felt Xavier take away my power, and this was no different. The air was taken out of my balloon, and I deflated as I took each step on the way back to my car.

A couple of silent weeks later, I met up with Xavier so that Tyler could visit for the weekend. We peacefully exchanged our child, but I couldn't help but still have this lingering feeling about our encounter. A piece of my heart was left in the guest bedroom that day. As I grappled with the reality that X didn't want my ass anymore, another curveball was tossed my way. Mother Nature decided to not show up.

"Shit!" I yelled from the bathroom. "Are you freaking kidding me?" I struggled to read another positive pregnancy test.

I was unexpectedly pregnant and in another complicated situation. I was beginning to doubt my ability to make sound choices. Xavier was getting ready to move cross-country for military work with his girlfriend in tow. I was contently paying a mortgage, raising our daughter, and building a business that was taking up most of my time. *Why now, Lord?*

Xavier badgered me over the phone for an hour about my pregnancy and how I was ruining his life. I wasn't completely sure what I wanted to do. I was so confused, but I did know that I was not going to let him bully me into a decision. He had no clue what I'd gone through the year prior, and neither would he particularly care. His only concern was not having to pay for another child.

I spent seventy-two hours mulling over and praying about this twisted circumstance. In all my thinking, one thing became clear: I would become the mother of two. As much as I had feared Xavier's reaction, I made sure to tell this man face-to-face about the decision I'd made without him.

"It's a nice day." I walked up to Xavier as he waited for me at the edge of Sunset Cliffs, where we'd had our first date years ago. "I'm happy the rain is gone."

It was crazy that I was having the exact conversation I'd had with Kalvin a year prior. Except this time, I was making the decision.

"Thanks for meeting me. I know that our last conversation was heated, and I totally get your feelings." I took a deep breath. "I'm scared too."

Xavier stood outside of his car, staring at the crushing summer waves. He finally turned toward me and made eye contact. "You totally get my feelings? Evidently you don't. What? Are you about to tell me that you don't believe in abortion?" he said.

"I am trying to be a woman about the situation. We laid down, and a baby came out of it. Evidently this was supposed to—"

"Please don't say this was supposed to happen. That is not fate. This is you trying to ruin my life!"

"Look, I am not going to take this verbal lashing. You are grown. I am grown. You stuck your penis inside of me, so take responsibility for that!" Xavier had no control over what was happening, and he didn't like feeling out of control. I pressed my point despite the fact that I saw the energy shifting from bad to worse. "I know you have a little girlfriend and have plans to leave soon. You can figure out how to deal with that. As for me? I'm handling my business. I'm having this child."

"Fuck you, Brooklen. Fuck you and everything about you. Good luck. You're on your own."

Xavier continued his verbal lashing in an attempt to degrade me for my decision. He kept pushing me. He wanted me to abort. I walked toward my car in order to escape his punishment. This was already a difficult situation for me, and he was adding extreme insult to injury. I managed to safely get into my car and get the hell off Sunset Cliffs before I ended up in the ocean.

Truth be told, when a man lies down with a woman, he is making his choice right then and there to potentially become a parent with that woman. A man may feel voiceless when a woman decides to follow through with a pregnancy against his will, but where was his voice when her legs were open, giving him loads of pleasure? Granted, we already had one child, which made the decision slightly easier for me. And most important, I had a promise that I'd made to God, and I wasn't going to break it because of situational inconvenience.

Most of the 280 days of my pregnancy was spent crying in a puddle of self-pity. I felt so much guilt bringing a child into an unstable situation, and that bothered me. I didn't want to be single and doing this alone, but

I had to lie in the bed that I made. In addition, Xavier made the move across the country with his girlfriend while I prepared for the birth of his second—well, technically, his third—child to be born. The onset of depression crept up on me at least weekly, and it was an ongoing fight to beat off that demon.

Midway through my pregnancy, I began fearlessly journaling to release my obsessive thoughts and pain. Journaling became lifesaving therapy in my poor, little, hormonal world. I'd write to "tell" Xavier the things I couldn't tell him face-to-face. My journal was a safe place to express my authentic and raw emotion without judgment or receiving unsolicited advice.

> November 3, 2008. As I lie here on this uncomfortable ass mattress, I am disgusted by my choices this year. I would never tell you this, but our situation reminds me of the paternity episodes on daytime television. How in the heck did I end up on this path? Well, I know why I ended up on this path: fear. The fear that you would truly move on with someone other than me led me to lie down with you that day. I subconsciously trapped you. Fear pushed my will to have you just one more time. I wanted to prove to myself that you still wanted me and that I could still have you. Then you once again rejected me in the midst of intercourse. I felt like shit. You took me into your arms and within minutes discarded me emotionally and physically. That moment in the guest bedroom has changed my life. Damn, look at how that plan backfired. Who is the one lying in bed alone, while you lie in bed with the woman you are choosing right now? I guess I will balance out my feelings of worthlessness once you or your girlfriend respond to those sonogram photos I put in the mail of our baby yesterday. Her heartbreak will hopefully relieve the battle in my heart for a moment. Yeah, eye for an eye, I guess …

Journals upon journals were filled with painful conversations with God, Xavier, and myself. The therapy of writing probably saved me from becoming a young stroke victim. The release of my suffocated frustration ended up opening up space for a very important conversation.

One day as I fought for comfort in my final trimester, Xavier called me. "Hey Brook, I know we've been talking more lately, and you know my current situation has changed."

I sat up on my bed to get a closer listen.

"With that being said, I'd like to come and see you."

"Wow. See me? Really?"

"Yeah. The baby will be here soon, and I've been thinking. Why don't we talk about working it out?" I sat on the phone in silence. "I plan to be there next week."

I responded positively to Xavier's idea. The thought that I may not have to do this alone relieved my soul.

Xavier arrived at San Diego airport on a mission to get his family back. With very few words exchanged about our complicated situation, we almost naturally started acting like a couple. He grabbed my hand as we walked back to my car from the airport terminal, as if he was reassuring me that we were in this together. I received the subtle sensation that traveled from my hand to my heart as confirmation. Furthermore, I was sure the energy from Xavier's touch activated my labor, because hours later I was checked in at Sharp Memorial Hospital, ready to give birth.

"Shut the front door! We got a baby coming!" shouted the energetic and seasoned nurse who prepped my delivery.

"Oh my God, this is happening now?" I responded in shock, although I wasn't in much pain because of the epidural administered shortly before. The pulsating pressure between my legs was a strong indication that I'd be pushing sooner rather than later.

My hospital room was filled with about fifteen of my closest friends and family members. Everyone scurried out of the room and into the hallway in anticipation of the new arrival. Left to preview the birth were Xavier, Cali, and Carol.

"Okay, Brooklen, the baby's head is crowning. Can you feel anything?" asked Dr. Khan, a middle-aged Indian woman with the softest hands that I'd ever felt. My baby was in good hands—literally.

"I feel some pressure but no pain. Do you want to push now, Doctor?"

"Yes, and once you push, your baby girl will be here."

A myriad of emotion consumed me as I thought about the recent months of strife that were coming to an end. My second baby girl was just moments away from her debut. Xavier stood by my side with his hand in mine. We watched our second child miraculously enter the world, and nothing else mattered. In that moment, we were family. In that moment, all darkness became light.

"Brooklen, give me a nice, hard push on the count of one … two … three."

A few firm pushes later, I gave birth to one of the most beautiful human beings on earth. Our second daughter was healthy and perfect from head to toe with gorgeous, dark, curly locks and deep ocean blue eyes. How did we make such a marvelous creation in the midst of such a relational chaos? Only God could turn this mess into a blessing. What seemed like a bad choice had become redeemed instantly. My redemption came in the form of the newest little Sapphire: Destiny.

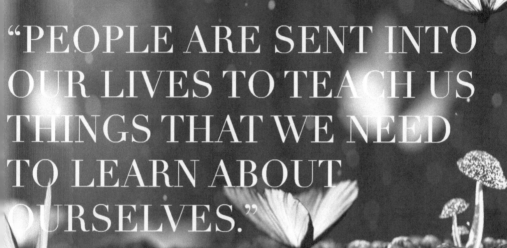

"PEOPLE ARE SENT INTO OUR LIVES TO TEACH US THINGS THAT WE NEED TO LEARN ABOUT OURSELVES."

Mandy Hale

Chapter 16

Stick It Out, Girl

People are sent into our lives to teach us things
that we need to learn about ourselves.
— Mandy Hale

Destiny Sapphire was everything her name suggested. Her new life produced a holy experience in my mind, body, and soul. She looked like my mother's mother. The Irish blood was prominent in her features from the almond milk skin to the deep indigo blue eyes. Destiny's features were a sight to behold.

The contrast between our second daughter's arrival and my emotional state was night and day. Admittedly, I didn't want to raise these babies alone, but going back to what we'd had in our marriage terrified me. Unfortunately, sitting on the fence was getting me nowhere, and Xavier's proposal to reconcile was still on the table. About five weeks after Destiny's birth, Xavier hopped on a plane back to New York to take care of all his unfinished personal business. We spent the following months fervently rebuilding our relationship, plus several thousands of dollars on cross-country flights. I felt it was time to make the move, but not without addressing a few things first.

"I need to make sure that I am not wasting time moving across the globe," I warned him. "I know that I asked before, but I just need to hear it again. Is that ex-girlfriend of yours anywhere in the picture?"

"Look, I already told you that I got my own place, and I don't see her anymore. Do you think I would be moving you out here if I wasn't telling the truth?"

"Do you really want me to answer that?"

"I don't need your sarcasm, Brooklen. Why do you always feel the need to ruin shit?"

X blamed me in every disagreement. We were falling back into the negative pattern of our old relationship, but I continued the quest for the family that I always wanted. Over the next few years, I had become a professional at ignoring the warning signs within our relationship. Simple disagreements would turn into full-on arguments or prolonged silent treatment. The emotional dance that we were so used to doing was falling right back into place, even in our phone conversations.

"And you sure know how to ruin a relation—"

"Bottom line, the past is in the past. Either you're going to trust me or you're not," Xavier cut me off with his final point.

"You can't expect me to just forget everything we've gone through. Trust takes time to rebuild."

The attempt to rebuild our relationship revealed how much brokenness still existed between us. One of the things that helped me overlook our discrepancies was his excitable love toward our newest daughter, Destiny. She brought out a side of him that I had never seen. He connected with her in a very special way. His desire to be there for our girls was all I needed to take back my family. I packed up my kids and moved across the country with 100 percent belief that I was doing the right thing for all of us.

Our peaceful stay on the East Coast was abruptly ended by an emergency military order for Xavier to return to San Diego. Eleven months later, we packed up our little life outside of Albany, New York, and returned home.

"I'm not happy about moving back home," I shared with Xavier.

We took down what were the beginning stages of the decor in our bedroom. I had a life planned for us there. San Diego represented so much struggle, and Albany was a chance for something better.

I continued, "Moving back is so bittersweet. I know we will have help with the girls and all, but there was something about being away that made us stronger."

"Well, I can't wait to get back to San Diego. I never liked it here."

This was another demonstration of how we were two rockets in desperate need of a course correction. I was loving the East Coast, and he was dying to get back home. I believed he missed the familiarity and comfort of his friends, family, and the streets. His identity was still in San Diego.

Xavier had ties to his street friends, and I never truly understood that dynamic. They always seemed to bring out a side of him that left a poor taste in my mouth. I liked the man who was funny, affectionate, and ultrasensitive with our daughters. I wanted to keep that man intact, but moving back home meant that I was going to have to face the street thug that periodically resurfaced and irritated the hell out of me. His sleeping beast was usually at bay until the Skyline streets picked at it and prodded for it to awaken. That beast was my nemesis.

The following night, Xavier, Destiny, Tyler, and I took a red-eye flight back to SoCal. We arrived the next morning to a crisp Monday sunrise, baby blue skies, and loads of flip-flop-wearing San Diegans.

"Home, sweet home," Xavier proudly announced.

I stood behind him in the airport rolling my eyes behind my Raybans. "Ain't nothin' sweet about being back here," I mumbled under my breath as we shuffled to baggage claim.

"Did you say something?" Xavier questioned.

"Huh, me? Oh, no, I didn't say a thing." I was such a horrible liar. "Let's just get our stuff and head to the place. I'm beat."

We arrived at our new apartment nestled in the hills of Clairemont Mesa, a quaint neighborhood in the central region of San Diego that had a healthy mix of military retirees and young families. The spacious, two-bedroom had some great kitchen upgrades, a patio overlooking the community pool, and all the convenient amenities. The girls were jumping up and down at the sight of our new digs, and their smiles gave me hope that maybe this wouldn't be so bad.

The first few months back home were a breeze. They were so good that we started to entertain the idea of marriage for the second time. Our short time in New York helped us build a foundation for our relationship. I felt our bond was stronger than ever. We communicated more often, nipped our disagreements in the bud, and focused on our family. The plan to reconcile was looking like a great decision.

It was the summer 2010, and Xavier's six-month deployment was quickly approaching. The preparation for his departure was always so stressful, whether we were figuring out how to save the tax-free income while he was overseas or coming up with a new daily routine. Anxiety crept into my mind because I was worried whether he would be able to remain faithful. Our foundation seemed stronger, but would it withstand this much time away? Would he fall weak in a tempting moment and betray me? I did my best to curb the negative thoughts and stay positive, but I couldn't ignore this nagging voice telling me that something was up.

One afternoon while Tyler and Destiny were away at school, I pulled up a chair to our dining room table to pay some bills online. Our cell phone bill was first. I normally never paid attention to the call details, but this time something told me to take a look. There were several calls throughout the day, for days at a time, for long durations. The longer calls seemed to happen right around the time Xavier got off work.

"What in the hell?"

My mind jumped to every negative conclusion. I felt a jolting spike in my blood pressure, and I began scrolling for more evidence. The only way to ease my mind was to find out to whom this phone number belonged.

"Yeah, hello?" My palms sweated and my hands trembled as I prepared to question the hell out of this woman.

"Who is this?" The other voice on the phone sounded like a nasty, ghetto chick. I sized her up over the phone in a millisecond. He was definitely screwing her.

"You don't know me, but your number is on my phone bill. Do you know an Xavier?"

The dial tone penetrated my eardrum almost instantly. This chick hung up and never answered again. Who in the hell was she? And what did she have to hide? Without hesitation I called Xavier to interrogate him with the research that I'd found, but he didn't answer the phone. Go figure. I hit the end button on my cell phone like I was trying to end someone's life.

The moment that I got ready to build more investigative ammo, Mr. Xavier King walked in the front door. Perfect timing. "Hey, Brook. What's up?"

I stared at him in disgust. X shuffled into the house with his work bag and bulky uniform. He took off his combat boots and tossed them under the entertainment center as I sat and watched his every lying, cheating-ass move.

"So, whose number is this, Xavier?" I couldn't even fathom faking small talk. "I see for the past few weeks you've been having extended conversations at what looks like the exact time you get off work."

Xavier worked on a military base across San Diego's historic Coronado Bridge. I imagined his ass laughing and buttering up some random woman on the phone every day after work as he drove home to me. I could just see it. I really wanted to toss him over that bridge.

"Here you go. Always thinking the worst of somebody." Xavier was a professional question dodger. Either he was diminishing my claim or turning the questions around on me in order to divert my attention. I saw right through him every single time. The frustrating part was knowing that he was strategically avoiding my questions and would never answer me straight up.

"I'm not thinking the worst. I am simply asking a question. Would you like for me to call the number, and we can find out together?"

"Call the damn number! Do what the hell you want to do!" he shouted in defense.

What I wanted to do was find out more information about this woman who'd not only invaded my cell phone bill but also hung up on me. I could tell by his initial reaction that he wasn't going to tell me the truth. As soon as X lay down for a nap, my investigation ensued. I went back to look at our phone bill, and I pulled out the oldest trick in the book. I blocked my phone number and called the chick again. I noticed her ring tone played Kelly Rowland's "Motivation," which really pissed me off. It was crystal clear to me that this wasn't a professional relationship, and it definitely fed my thoughts of an affair.

"Who is this?"

"This is Brooklen, the wife of Xavier." We were divorced but together, so I was still the damned wife as far as I was concerned.

"Wife? He didn't say anything to me about a wife!"

I responded with a leading question in order to get the answer that I wanted. "So, you're basically telling me that you've been dealing with my man?"

"You need to talk to Xavier, not me." She hung up again.

I sat on my living room couch with my heart in the pit of my stomach. I was duped and betrayed.

About a week had gone by since the news of Xavier's mystery woman came out. He repeatedly attempted to turn things around on me whenever I brought up his slip in character. His body language showed remorse, but I still ended up feeling like a mother punishing her child for bad behavior. In a strange way, I was empathetic toward Xavier; his reverse psychology tactics were obviously working.

"I'm just going to end it all. You guys are better off without me," Xavier warned. "You'll be taken care of with almost half a million dollars in insurance money. I'm giving up. I'm so sorry this had to happen."

I read his text message while I sat in rush hour traffic, heading home from work. I immediately took the next exit and pulled over to take a closer look at what he was implying. My heart pounded in fear about what this coded message was *really* saying. I took a deep breath before responding.

"Xavier, what is going on?"

Our text messages went back and forth for about half an hour before I realized he was serious about taking his life. He spoke about ending it all, adding that we were better off without him. All of a sudden, X stopped responding. The silence was heart-wrenching as I sat overlooking the freeway traffic. Each second represented a dying moment that someone could have been saving him. I called him, and again there was no answer. I made one last effort to reach him via text. "Xavier, answer me. Please!"

I mentally stepped out the Xavier's drama and realized that my children needed to be picked up from school. I was in no condition to look at their precious faces. I couldn't imagine the horror if my children saw their dad lying dead on the floor. I called Naomi to ask if she'd pick up the girls until we got to the bottom of this.

Almost an hour had gone by, and still no response. I broke down and called 911. "I think my husband wants to kill himself. He sent me some specific text messages indicating that he was going to take his life. Can someone please go to my house and check on him—now?"

I drove to a Walmart store near Naomi's home, sat in my parked car, and waited for the cops to call back. I pulled out my cell phone and sent out an SOS text message for prayer to a few family members. Did this man really do it? Did he pull the trigger out of guilt? My worst fears filled my mind as I imagined how our lives would change without Xavier. I reclined in my driver's seat and closed my eyes.

"Lord, I don't know how we got here. I don't know what is going on in Xavier's mind. But please don't let him do something that we will all suffer from later. Can you protect him? Can you save him from himself? I trust that you will answer this prayer. In Jesus's name, amen."

After my prayer, I called Xavier's older brother, Big Kev, an ex-NFL player and the protector of the family. I asked him to drive out to my house and see if X had followed through with his threat. About fifteen minutes later, my phone received an incoming call from Big Kev.

"Brook, I just got here. The cops have X. He's okay."

My eyes closed, and a sigh of relief left my body. "Thank God," I said.

"Yeah, it looks like they are asking him some questions in your bedroom. Our prayers worked."

According to the authorities, they rang the doorbell to our apartment several times with no answer. They were forced to kick the door down in an attempt to save Xavier's life. The cops found him on his knees with his head in his hands, crying uncontrollably. It appeared to them that he was praying. Although I was relieved he was alive, a part of me found some satisfaction in his guilt.

The cops transported Xavier to the nearest military hospital to be evaluated by psychologists. Within a couple of hours, he was cleared to go home. At that point, I decided to stay away for a few days. I called Cali to crash at her place. She happily cleared out the extra bedroom of her downtown condo, and the girls and I had a little staycation amid the drama.

How convenient that Xavier managed to redirect the focus of his cheating to a suicide attempt. I went from wanting to push him over a bridge to consoling a broken man. I thought I was the victim here. Was I a complete idiot for feeling sorry for this man after he breached our trust? Nonetheless, I worked too hard and endured too much to just throw it all away. There had been too many sleepless nights and moments of sacrifice for me to let another woman come in and destroy my home. That wasn't going down, not without a fight.

"SOMETIMES GIVING
SOMEONE A SECOND
CHANCE IS LIKE
GIVING THEM AN EXTRA
BULLET FOR THEIR GUN
BECAUSE THEY MISSED
YOU THE FIRST TIME."

— For Shits and Giggles

Chapter 17

I Do, Part Two

Sometimes giving someone a second chance is like giving them an extra bullet for their gun because they missed you the first time.

—anonymous

Xavier's deployment was a couple of months underway, and I was doing my best to move past the drama. Consequently, the time and distance served as a Band-Aid over my wounded heart. Xavier put his best foot forward and communicated with us almost daily. The brief phone calls that he managed to squeeze in after military drills or his heartfelt emails were timely and picked up my spirits. Every attempt he made to communicate reassured me that his commitment to our family was intact.

"So, baby, I was thinking that you could fly out to Hawaii when my ship pulls in and have a mini vacation. Just me and you. And what do you think about getting married again while we are there?"

Married? In Hawaii? Now he was pulling out all the stops. I sat in silence for a few moments before responding. "Well, don't you think that'd be crazy for us to marry each other twice?"

"Or it could be a story of the high school sweethearts making their relationship work. Everyone loves us together, anyway."

The perceived pressure from friends and family definitely weighed on my choice to stay with Xavier. He knew I wanted our family together, and his talk of marriage was right up my alley. After all, I was always taught to believe that good women forgave their men after stepping out on them, because keeping the family together was priority. I wanted to be a good woman to Xavier even at the expense of my own dignity.

"Let's do it," I quickly replied, as if the offer would be removed from the table. "I'll start looking for flights."

Hawaii was quickly approaching, yet I still had unresolved trust issues. I believed that therapy may help me address my own emotional damage. I was introduced to an excellent therapist through one of my Bible study classmates. Dr. Stevens was extremely professional, but she was also a straight shooter. We talked about my mommy and daddy issues and discussed methods of self-care like journaling and setting aside quiet time with God. Dr. Stevens showed me how to process my feelings after infidelity, and she helped address some of poor patterns that I was repeating. I was always such a calm person and didn't realize I was embodying so much stress. I was on the path to healing and hoped that Xavier was doing the same while he was away. They say the heart grows fonder with distance, and my heart was definitely opening up to the idea of spending my life with him again. As a result, I began planning our second wedding ceremony.

"Hawaii is absolutely beautiful!" I shared with Xavier.

He picked me up from the Honolulu airport, and we headed to grab some authentic Hawaiian food at the Moku Kitchen to discuss our upcoming nuptials. Honolulu was paradise. I had never seen so much water, palm trees, and flip-flops in one place. The vibes of the island were welcoming, and love was in the air. It was the perfect place to have a wedding for two.

It had been six months since the last time we'd laid eyes on one another, and all we wanted to do was have sex and more sex. This was our first kid-free vacation, and there was no shortage of fun. Considering the year we had behind us, fun was definitely on the menu. We soaked up the greatness of Hawaii at ceremonial luaus, and we lay on breathtaking beaches. After a couple of days of romping around the city, we decided upon a quaint spot off the coast of Kapolei for our wedding ceremony.

"Wow, we are about to do it again. How do you feel?" I asked.

We walked along the sandy beach barefoot as the officiant followed closely behind. Our hands were interlocked, but my heart was anxious.

Where were these feelings coming from? Wedding day jitters, or a sign from up above?

"I'm feeling good, Brook. You?"

"I'm good."

I lied—I wasn't good. My feelings weren't the normal "I'm getting ready to marry my best friend, and I'm nervously excited to spend the rest of my life with him" jitters. It was fear of making the biggest mistake of my life once again.

I questioned everything, including the Pee Wee Herman–looking officiant I could barely take seriously.

"Brooklen, do you take Xavier to be your lawful wedded husband?" he asked in his awkward, high-pitched tone.

I was forcing myself down the aisle. No one was forcing me. I was forcing myself to do this with a cross-fingered, one-eye-opened prayer that things would be different this time around. I sucked it up and faced the music. I took a deep breath. "Yes, I do."

Xavier repeated his vows with the same look of uncertainty on his face. We struggled to even look each other in the eyes. We said our I-dos and played Russian roulette with our marriage. I hoped the one bullet didn't lay us out flat with no chance of resuscitation. We returned to San Diego after a few more days of fun in the sun.

It wasn't even a month into our second marriage that I started to feel insecure. It mirrored the feeling I'd had at the altar the first time almost nine years prior. I hoped Xavier would turn into the man I saw in my dreams: God-fearing, honest, loyal, and nothing short of amazing. The honest truth was that X was broken and hurt, like many men who refuse address their personal wounds. I married a broken-down dog and wanted to play Mrs. Veterinarian. I was over fifteen years deep into trying to cure someone without realizing I needed to be cured myself. Needless to say, it wasn't long after our return home that X reverted back to his old ways and cheated. Again.

There I was, feeling trapped. What sense would it make to file for divorce after just getting married? How would that look? Unfortunately, what others thought of me was another reason I stayed in my relationship. "Why am I putting up with this shit?" was the real question. Why was I enduring if it didn't feel right? I tried to justify my life by saying God allowed this pain for some greater purpose. Or was I choosing to stay in my dysfunction?

After all these years with X, I accepted that cheating, silent treatment, poor communication, and the overall nagging feeling of our relationship was normal. I thought most couples went through this, and that we would eventually get to the other side. All the pain that this relationship caused must have meant that there was some huge blessing on the other side, right? I couldn't have been going through all this for nothing. I thought I was experiencing the longsuffering that the Bible talked about. The pain of this relationship had become my norm, and I was convinced that sporadic moments of happiness were all I needed.

November 28, 2010

You never say I'm sorry. The past few weeks, you have treated me like I don't even matter. When I try to talk to you about it, it's this whole act of congress just to get you to engage! You don't care, and your actions and body language say so. The past three weeks have really put a damper on my trust in you. I don't know what's genuine or not. You disregard my feelings without a single care for them. You cheat like you're sick or something! What the hell is wrong with you? I would never treat you the way you treat me. I would never belittle your feelings, and I would never disrespect you the way you disrespect me. I feel extremely disconnected. And when we do connect, it's just a matter of time before we disconnect again. I feel that I'm going through the motions here. And you wonder why you don't know that I have these feelings inside? Because you never care enough to ask or listen.

December 1, 2010

Today, you told me how irresponsible I was because I'd miscalculated the daycare bill. You scolded me like a child and said how bad I was with money. A form of verbal abuse. I am going to look up the definition. I cannot talk to you, so I keep praying that something changes. I feel like I can't be myself with you, and I have to watch every tiny thing I say in fear that I have to deal with your wrath. This isn't healthy. It can't be. I want to do better, and I am unhappy. You say everything is my fault, and you never do wrong, which is why you never apologize. I know God has better for me. I am being patient and waiting for His signal, I guess … You are negative, mean, and selfish to your core. When you are nice, it is superficial and temporary. I try to love you in spite of your behavior, but like all your relationships with women, you feel that you don't need to make an effort. When I leave this journal to you, you will read it, saying that I was crazy, or that I thought I was perfect, or that I was too deep. The reality is that your life is a reflection of the effort you put into it. I guess succeeding in the military was all you cared about, because your personal relationships are shit.

Just call me Yvette from John Singleton's *Baby Boy*. I was dealing with a man-child with stifled emotional development who found his definition of manhood in all the chauvinistic examples displayed in urban American culture. I had forfeited my standards, my wants, and my needs in order to make my family work, and I was paying for it. I subconsciously believed that if I kept having babies, it would correct all the wrongs of the relationship. I knew, like so many other women that our children would hold us together, and temporarily they did. But the true turmoil that had set in our relationship would always resurface as time went on. How could I wholeheartedly love him and feel like I was running into a brick wall at the same time? I had accepted the pain of broken trust, but I still worked overtime to ensure his happiness over my own. I had officially spent the better part of my life loving and pouring myself into a man who wasn't capable of doing the same for me. I was in a one-sided marriage.

In my confusion, I started looking back at patterns and recalled some of the talks I'd had with Dr. Stevens. I realized that I had been crying about the same issues year after year. I was doing the same thing over and over, expecting a different result. I was insane! All my journal entries were about pain and drama with an occasional joyous moment. I prayed and cried, prayed and cried, and *he* was not changing. I made it my life purpose to be the praying wife who saw my husband through to the other side. The "other side" meaning that I would see him through to his healing and to the realization of his potential. Just call me the typical down-ass chick. I stayed loyal to a vision that I'd dreamt up in my own mind, and I let it continually drive me to stick out our relationship. I saw the same red flags that were there when I was fifteen, and nothing had changed. Why weren't my prayers working? Why didn't God want me to have the desires of my heart and the family that I envisioned? Maybe, just maybe, I was asking the wrong questions.

"GOD OPENS MILLIONS OF FLOWERS WITHOUT FORCING THE BUDS. IT REMINDS US NOT TO FORCE ANYTHING, FOR THINGS HAPPEN IN THE RIGHT TIME."

– *Nishan Panwar*

Chapter 18

Forcing a Square Peg into a Circle

God opens millions of flowers without forcing the buds. It reminds
us not to force anything, for things happen in the right time.
—Nishan Panwar

"Thank God for new beginnings. Our new place is amazing," I
shared with Xavier as we brought boxes into our 3,500-square-
foot home in the coastal community of Carlsbad, California.

We'd spent most of our lives living in the inner city and had finally
moved up. A few years had gone since our wedding on the beach in Hawaii.
We had experienced some seemingly positive changes in our marriage, we
had great career advancements, and we had healthy and happy children.

"We have come a long way, and this house is bomb!" he replied.

"I can't believe I am actually living near the water! I can see us taking
the girls on little beach dates and stuff ..."

"Well, you guys have fun with that. I'll be right here on this PlayStation."

And there was the trigger to my underlying marital sadness. Although
we were experiencing such a great time in life on the outside, I was still
struggling on the inside. I dreamed of family trips to the local farm,
whereas Xavier was focused on getting to his leather recliner and putting
a gaming controller in his hand. I continued to ignore my instincts by

focusing on the bigger picture. We were in a good place, and nothing seemingly threatened the weak spots in our marriage, so I didn't rock the boat. I simply put a smile on my face and acted happy with my life.

"I'm so sad that you have to leave again. We are just getting settling into the new place."

"Brook, you know I can't control with the military does. They said I have to go, and there is no way out of it."

"I get that. I'm just expressing my feelings. To have to take care of the girls in this big house all alone is depressing, that's all. But you are right. I guess I'll just suck it up."

Xavier showed minimal sympathy for others, and I was no exception. Tyler and Destiny probably got the most out of him emotionally, but even that appeared limited.

"Well, before we move from this topic of you leaving, I need to share something else with you."

"What's up?"

"You know how I took a break from my birth control while you went out to do drills on the water for thirty days?" I geared up to drop the scariest bomb.

"Yeah," he stated in a dry tone.

"I took a test. It was positive."

Xavier's face rose in irritation as I stood nervously anticipating his response.

"What the hell do you mean, it was positive? Did you do this shit on purpose?"

"Hell, no! I told you before I was taking a break from those pills. I hated taking them, and we weren't having sex because you were gone!" I felt the blame creeping in because Xavier never wanted to take responsibility. "Why would I get pregnant on purpose, knowing you didn't want any more kids? I mean, damn, I'm your wife. Where is the support?"

"To hell with your support. This just means more money out of my pocket."

My husband's rejection was a blow to the gut. Xavier rarely responded the way I wanted or needed. The next nine months proved to be my loneliest pregnancy to date. As my body grew, Xavier and I grew further apart. He then ceased any and all physical displays of affection, and this included sex. I felt unwanted, unloved, and less of a woman because of his wrath. And like a puppy, I awaited Xavier's approval and desired him beyond comprehension. The only thing I felt could redeem this situation was if I was carrying his dream.

"It's a girl!" the sonographer joyfully shared.

"Are you sure?" I asked. Hearing these words were my worst nightmare. I wanted to have X's legitimate son.

"Well, typically when we spot the 'hamburger,' we know it's a girl. The 'hot dog' will let us know we are looking at a boy."

"Is there any way that you can double-check? I was so sure I was having a boy. This pregnancy is totally different that my other two."

The sonographer rubbed my belly with gel and went in for another look. I closed my eyes and prayed. *Lord, please give me my son. Please.*

Within seconds I got an answer to that prayer. It just wasn't the one that I wanted.

"Yes, we definitely have ourselves a girl," the sonographer confidently stated.

I picked my broken heart up off the floor, walked outside of the medical facility, and sat in the driver's seat of my car. I dropped my head and began crying like a disappointed child who didn't get her most desired toy for Christmas. It took months for my gender disappointment to diminish, because the little boy that I'd envisioned wasn't coming. A side chick gave my husband a son, and I felt she'd won. I somehow felt that a boy child would not only rectify the situation but also make me feel good. I wanted to feel good about something, and most of all, I wanted to feel good about saving this marriage.

My disappointment over the fact that we were not having a son was met with extreme insensitivity from Xavier. He'd get frustrated at my fragile emotions around the topic and say things like, "Get over it," or, "We just weren't meant to have a son." His insensitivity caused me to question myself and God. After all, I was doing everything right, and God couldn't find it inside to grant me this one desire. I would have done just about anything for those sonograms to be wrong. Letting go of the son I desired was one of the hardest things I ever had to do.

"CAUGHT IN A DREAM OF WHERE I WANT TO BE WRAPPED IN A WEB OF WHERE I AM."

— *Michael W. Smith*

Chapter 19

Out of the Blue Sea

Caught in a dream of where I want to be
wrapped in a web of where I am.
—Michael W. Smith

Our third daughter, Selah Dream, was born at a healthy seven pounds, three ounces on the most perfect Sunday a couple of days shy of my father's birth date in June 2014. Selah, like her sisters, came out perfectly healthy with those dreamy eyes that were prominent in Xavier's family. She was such calm and easygoing baby, and I felt blessed to have her join our tribe. My old dream was replaced with the sweetest aroma of a newborn baby girl.

Xavier walked in from work one day with the sourest look on his face. I had spent the day dropping off and picking up girls from school, breast-feeding, changing diapers, and planning a meal for dinner. I too felt like I'd put in an eight-hour shift, and I still had a few more to go.

"What's up, X? How was your day?"

"These assholes want to send us on a ten-month deployment!"

"What?" I was pissed. "We just celebrated you making chief, we have a four-week-old newborn, and you have to go?"

Xavier's new position put him in the upper echelon of the military. Our lives had completely changed. As a spouse, I had to befriend new people and even read handbooks on etiquette. Although I embraced the new role, I wasn't happy about Xavier having to leave us so soon. I had three children and feared facing the extra responsibility all alone.

"My promotion will guarantee that I have to go. They will need the leadership."

"The timing is horrible," I affirmed. "Well, I guess you'll have to bond with Selah as much as you can. You'll miss her whole first year."

In the midst of our excitement around his new job, I noticed that X seemed a little disconnected from our newest daughter. Now that there was a pending deployment, he shared that it was better to not bond with her. That confused me. He figured that there was no sense in getting close to her if he'd have to leave. I guessed that was his attempt to soften any blow. I tried to be understanding, but something about his deliberate disconnection made me uneasy. Each and every day, my anxiety grew knowing that the inevitable was going to happen. He'd be gone on a ship across the world while I was left to raise three children. Deployments almost felt like divorce and affected everyone connected to them.

Within weeks, Xavier was shipped off to another part of the world, and I was left to fill the shoes of mom and dad. I started to suffer from a serious case of postpartum anxiety. The reality of being left alone to raise and protect our three girls didn't sit well with me. I had many sleepless nights as I worried about someone breaking into our home, or someone taking my children. I even visualized the world coming to an end. I had considered calling Dr. Stevens again, but making the time and arrangements to see her seemed overwhelming. Fortunately, due to constant prayer and mommy breaks, the postpartum dissipated within six months of Selah's birth. The sunshine was pouring in again, but not without a storm on the horizon.

"I think we should get a divorce," Xavier stated in an email about six months into his ten-month tour.

My mouth dropped in sheer bafflement. I responded to his email with an onslaught of questions. "You want a what? Wait. Where is this coming from? There must be another woman! Are you just homesick and becoming insecure? What's really going on?" Not only did I ask him these questions, but I repeated these crappy imaginings in my head.

Finally, after three days, Xavier replied. "I've just had a lot of time to think. This ain't working, and we've only been staying together for the kids."

He supposedly had an epiphany one day out on the deck of the ship. Was he gazing at the water one night while a woman was rubbing his penis, and it just hit him that he didn't want to be a husband anymore? I questioned where this was coming from, and I wasn't buying the shit. I knew there was a bitch lurking somewhere. It simply didn't sound right, and I was going to continue to dig until the truth came out.

My mind raced as I recalled how great things seemed to be just before he'd left: new promotion, new baby, and happy family—or so I thought. I felt bamboozled. I mentally prepared for his return, yet I didn't know where our marriage stood and how I would even manage having X around again. A part of me was in complete denial because he had thrown the D word around so many times in the past that I truly didn't know whether he meant it. Whenever he felt threatened within the relationship, he would push me away and then reel me back in by uttering the word divorce. This control tactic worked on me for years, and it was working again. Not only was I mentally off my game due to this man crying wolf, but the ten months without him was also taking its toll on me. A deployment can do some real damage to a marital bond, especially when that bond has already been weakened by breaches of trust. I was stuck processing a potential divorce and welcoming a man back home who didn't want me anymore.

Our relationship status had officially become complicated. The last few months of his tour consisted of me trying to figure out the matrix of X. He appeared to be sticking to his guns, but was he serious this time?

"Welcome home, Daddy," read the sign our girls made as we greeted him at the San Diego International Airport.

"Daddy, Daddy!" the girls screamed as they raced through the walkways.

The color of emotions I felt were indescribable as I looked at my husband for the first time in almost ten months. *Do I kiss him? What do I say?*

"Hey, babies! Daddy has missed you so much," Xavier said to the girls while he cut me with the side-eye from hell.

"Damn, what did I do to you?" I asked. That was exactly the problem. I rarely did anything to deserve this treatment. Xavier dismissed me like the latest celebrity hot topic, and I took it. I took it for my family. "Welcome home," I stated under my breath in a tone of sacasm. I continued to trail behind X and the girls while my confused emotions tried to assemble themselves.

A few days passed since his return home, and I knew that I was dealing with a different man. I could tell that being overseas had changed him. I watched him struggle mentally, and his extreme lack of emotional availability was a surefire sign that something wasn't the same. He was a shell of himself, and the sad truth was that I was in this alone.

Xavier began reverting back to his unfavorable habits of late-night hanging out and living a single man's life. It was excruciating, watching him as a grown man be involved in hood drama with friends from the past. I wondered why would someone with his prestige in the military wasted time speaking Ebonics and prided himself in helping his friends solve their problems. I felt he craved attention and acceptance from the wrong people. All the while, he had a hurting wife at home who was yearning for a loving touch, some intimacy, or a simple conversation!

A few months into his adjustment back home, we still hadn't taken the time to discuss the state of our marriage. My cup was soon to spill over.

September 25, 2015

I feel frustrated with this marriage. You have ignited a roller coaster of emotion by stating that you want a divorce back in February, but you won't talk to me about it! You won't have sex with me and only God knows why! I feel that you don't even try to push up on me! How about just sleeping in the bed together? Can we do that? Just once? Hanging out with your friends always gets you excited, which is nothing new; I always felt that you had more loyalty to them. Getaways, clubs—you have been willing to make time for those things. I deserve to be considered. The lack of effort to take care of me shows me that you don't want to be in this marriage. You're not caring for it. It's more important for you to be a good homie than it is for you to be a good husband. The fact that you have time to solve your boys' problems but not the problems in your home is beyond me. I really don't deserve this shit.

I got really good at writing out my bottled-up emotions to keep from going insane. Between managing the kids, starting a new business, and trying to take care of myself, this one-sided marriage was adding an unnecessary thorn in my side. The sad part was that things only got worse between us. The wedge that the deployment created added to the countless challenges that we already faced. I was so ready to tap out. As tears streamed down my face, I realized that the vicious cycle of feeling loved and unloved was coming to a head. Everything that I had been experiencing over the years finally prompted me to take to the internet. I went to Google and searched *emotional abuse.*

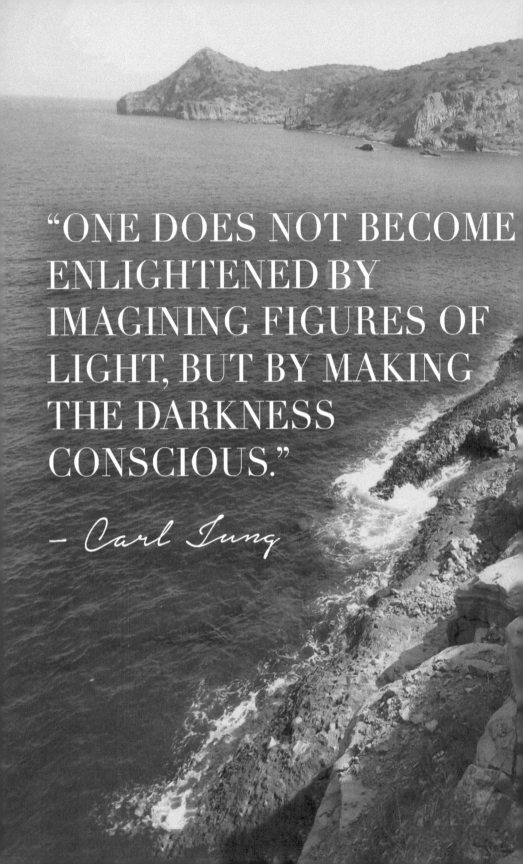

"ONE DOES NOT BECOME ENLIGHTENED BY IMAGINING FIGURES OF LIGHT, BUT BY MAKING THE DARKNESS CONSCIOUS."

— Carl Jung

Chapter 20

Darkness to Light

One does not become enlightened by imagining figures
of light, but by making the darkness conscious.
—Carl Jung

I read countless articles, stories, and medical reports on emotional abuse. I realized that not only had I been in an abusive relationship, but I had been dealing with a possible narcissist! Xavier mirrored many of the documented traits, such as having a superiority complex, extreme selfishness, childlike behavior, and desire for unreasonable amounts of attention with little to no regard for others, among others. He was a deeply wounded man and had acquired great skill over his lifetime creating a fake persona to hide his truth and mask the pain. This persona kept his ego afloat as he tried to maintain a normal life. Xavier was an obsessive overachiever, was a lover of flashy things, and was quite compulsive about keeping his outer appearance up—all signs pointing toward this disorder. Although I knew I couldn't diagnose him with any mental conditions, I realized that this may have been what I'd been dealing with. I realized that I wasn't crazy, and there was indeed rhyme and reason to this roller coaster I was on. After countless nights researching, I realized that I was a victim of emotional abuse. The only way to remotely life a happy life was to walk away from this unhealthy situation.

One evening, I cleaned up the kitchen after dinner and laid the girls down to bed. I made sure to plan this important conversation with X because it became very important to strategize our communication. If I opened up a conversation at the wrong time, chances were I wouldn't get the answers that I needed. So there I was, trying again.

"We haven't spoken in almost two months. When are you going to give this up?"

Silence.

"Xavier, I am not talking to a wall!" I cried. "Our kids are seeing you treat their mother like a piece of crap every single day. Is that what you want?"

Silence.

"You need help. I can't keep living like this. Our kids deserve better. I deserve better!"

More silence.

Xavier straight up ignored me while playing videos games. That was the norm, or he'd exaggeratedly direct his attention to one of our children as a way to dig his knife of hate deeper into me. There were so many days over the years that I walked on eggshells to keep the peace. Even while having to endure the serial silent treatment, I still chased after him. Chased him to answer me, chased him to spend time with me, and chased him to have sex with me. Chased, chased, chased! I was tired. I begged the Lord to give me a way out.

The year was coming to a close, and there was much to reflect on in my life and the lives of my children. Even in the inevitability of my marital demise, it was important for me to stay positive for my three girls. Tyler and Destiny had grown into beautiful overachievers during these rough years in my marriage to Xavier; I was grateful that they didn't seem too affected by our turmoil. Tyler was a rising student athlete on the junior varsity basketball team, and Destiny lived out her name and started her modeling and acting career. Selah was developing beautifully as we approached her second birthday. In all the pain, there was sunshine in the faces of my children.

On this rainy day in Southern California, I was at home doing my usual cleaning while Xavier was on duty for work. Selah was peacefully napping, and I went into Destiny's room to fold laundry. On her bed I found an iPod that I knew belonged to X. Destiny had been playing with it the day before. Wow, no passcode? The thing was unlocked. Now, I always heard from "mature" women that if you go snooping around, you may find something you don't like. The fact of the matter was that I didn't like my life, so a way out was actually what I was looking for. This iPod could lead me to intel on my husband's crisis! I had not had a genuine conversation with him since he'd returned from deployment. Maybe, just maybe, I'd get some answers out of this iPod.

> From: John Doe
> Sent: Friday, March 27, 2015 2:06 PM
> To: Kerianne Simpson
> Subject: RE: I miss you …
> Baby, the way you put it down the other night was like *damn*! I love you so much …

> From: Kerianne Simpson
> Sent: Friday, March 27, 2015 2:36 PM
> To: John Doe
> Subject: RE: I miss you …
> Baby, I love you too. You weren't so bad yourself. So, are you going to buy me those shoes I sent to you?

> From: John Doe
> Sent: Friday, March 27, 2015 3:16 PM
> To: Kerianne Simpson
> Subject: RE: I miss you …
> Send me the website again. I'll get you anything you want, baby. What's your mailing address?

> From: Kerianne Simpson
> Sent: Friday, March 27, 2015 2:36 PM
> To: John Doe
> Subject: RE: I miss you …
> Time can't go by fast enough until we see each other again. I love you …

Here's my address:
789 Mistress Court
New York, New York 10002

And there was my way out. I'd asked God for a sign, and damn it, I got one. Without a second thought, I trusted my gut and decided to leave my marriage. I decided that enough was enough. I decided that Xavier would never be able to hurt me like this again. I didn't even need an explanation of the affair, because all my answers came in a string of emails from Kerianne Simpson. Kerianne wasn't the bad guy; X used her like he did all the others. She wasn't a threat to me—none of the women were. Xavier was my threat, but only if I continued to stay.

"SHE HAD NOT KNOWN
THE WEIGHT UNTIL SHE
FELT THE FREEDOM."

– *Nathaniel Hawthorne*

Chapter 21

A Time for Freedom

She had not known the weight until she felt the freedom.
—Nathaniel Hawthorne

After my discovery, I left the unlocked iPod on our kitchen countertop with the email messages open. I wanted Xavier to know that I knew without a confrontation. Of course, his silence continued, and I allowed twenty-four hours to pass before approaching him. Our talk was an utter failure because he wouldn't open his damn mouth. It was almost like dealing with a second grader. My mute husband had no balls to stand up and tell me the truth. Xavier neither confirmed nor denied the affair, but the emails were all the proof I needed.

Over the next few weeks, our home felt like a desolate wasteland. Our painfully quiet home pierced my soul like knives and devastated our girls. I began spending hours a day planning my departure from Xavier. As a stay-at-home mom, my resources were very limited. I hadn't worked since Selah's birth. X locked me out of all the bank accounts and cut off my access to his paycheck. I was forced to live off credit cards and take out personal loans to keep afloat among the influx of bills. The next step in my plan to depart was getting back to work.

One day as I sat on my laptop searching for jobs, my doorbell unexpectedly rang.

"Hello, how can I help you?"

There was a delivery guy with a clipboard standing in front of me, looking rushed, as if he was trying to get to his next drop-off.

"Um, what is this?" I asked.

"I have a delivery for Xavier," he uttered.

"Okay, what are you delivering?"

"I have a couple of couches, a bedroom, and a dining room set."

What in the hell? Why was X ordering furniture? I asked the delivery man to hold on for a minute while I gave Xavier a call.

"Of course you didn't answer your phone, so I had to leave a message," I began my voice mail message on Xavier's cell phone. "There is a man here trying to deliver furniture. What the hell is this stuff for? Call me back."

I walked back to the front door to sign the invoice. Two men began bringing in the delivery as I watched from the bedroom, feeling confused.

Surprisingly, Xavier responded with a text. "Don't touch my stuff. I am taking it with me when I leave for Florida. Do what you want with the old furniture."

Wow. So Xavier was moving to Florida, and this was how I find out about it? Classic. It reminded me of how I found out about his illegitimate son via an overheard phone conversation. Xavier could never directly communicate with me; it was always a roundabout way of delivery important news. I believed he didn't respect me enough to keep me informed. Our relationship consisted of constant guessing at what was happening in his world. Another reason to keep planning my departure.

As reality set in on all the upcoming changes, Xavier grew angered and even showed signs that he'd cause physical harm. One evening he almost knocked me over as we passed each other in the hallway. Another night, he punched a hole in our bedroom wall when I asked him to pay a bill. His hate was brewing toward me, and I had to get out of there. That same night, once X fell asleep, I pulled up the courthouse website on my laptop and began filling out the dissolution forms. Within twenty-four hours, I was standing in front of the San Diego courthouse feeling the déjà vu of this process all over again.

As I rode the elevator with my baby in tow, I prayed for God's favor that this process would go smoothly. I needed this to get done today and not a day later. I knew there would be some challenges bringing a baby along, but at the end of the day, I had to do what I had to do. I even wore the same clothes that I slept in the night before in an effort to save time and get to the courthouse early. I rode up the escalator with Selah on my hip, God in my heart, and a mission to accomplish.

"Brooklen Sapphire, please come to Window A."

My name was called by a very young-looking clerk, and I wondered whether her expertise was up to par. "I'm here to drop off a dissolution packet. Can you review it to make sure that I filled out everything properly?"

I handed the clerk my packet, and she began to verify the submitted information while Selah squirmed and pulled at my breasts for a snack.

"You will need to correct all of the highlighted areas and come back to me at the front of the line."

Just great. I figured there would be some things that needed correction, but to have to fill these forms out carefully with a one-year-old in tow was no easy feat. I almost wanted to walk away and come back another day, but I realized that I would only be prolonging the process if I got impatient.

As the new clerk began inputting my information into the system, she noticed a hiccup. "Brooklen, it seems that you already have a divorce case open."

"Okay, well, how is that possible? Did he file before me?"

According to the clerk, our first divorce case, which was opened over four years ago, was still pending. If this was the case, I'd have to go to the original courthouse where I'd filed to close the case and come back to open a new one. Shit.

"What? So I was never divorced the first time? I'm so confused."

"Let me double-check something ..." The clerk began typing in my information and switching between computer screens to determine whether this was an error. Was this curveball really about to knock me off my mission today? By the look on her face, I could tell she probably wouldn't have good news for me. At this point, I knew things were out of my control. If my prior divorce case was still open, then maybe that meant that I was supposed to stay married? While I waited, I began to pray to God.

And just like that, a seemingly more seasoned clerk walked up to Window A. "Hello. It looks like your case is showing open where you originally filed, back in 2006. Good news: your case was closed, and we will be using the same case number to open a file today."

I was so emotional after finally mustering the courage to file these papers, and for a moment it looked like it wasn't going to happen. Then in the blink of an eye, God turned it around. "You are an angel. If you only knew what it took for me to get here today. Thank you."

I packed up Selah in her stroller, left my corrected papers at the front desk, and walked out of the courthouse victorious. On the verge of Domestic Violence Awareness Month, I had finally made the decision to leave an emotionally abusive relationship that some would have encouraged me to stay in simply because my scars weren't physical. I knew what I had endured, and I knew that God released me from my marriage. Once the storm stopped raging in my mind, I was able to see that being emotionally manipulated wasn't God's plan for me.

My departure from Xavier was filled with guilt and relief at the same time. I felt relief for me and guilt for my children. One of my crutches in staying so long was the fact that I wanted to correct the wrongs of my parents' past. Although my parents' choices had nothing to do with my current situation, I carried the burden of wanting to do better than they had, by any means necessary. Yes, their choices affected me, but they should not have controlled me. Their choices didn't define me, but I allowed them to for years. When my dad left when I was six years old, it devastated my emotional growth and confidence as a young girl. I wanted so badly to prevent that feeling of powerlessness from happening to my children. I constantly looked for love and acceptance because the first man in my life who was supposed to give it to me hadn't done so for whatever reason. I lost my virginity at twelve, slept with grown men while I was underage, dabbled in recreational drugs before I left middle school, and dated stone-cold thugs. These bad boys I dated represented the father figure I was seeking, but like myself, they were also hurt souls, and I attracted them. That magnetic attraction bred only pain and incorrect habits in love. I realized that I wasn't the culprit, but indeed I was a participant in the abuse because I'd allowed it. Once the bright light of awareness hit me, I was able to walk out of my outwardly beautiful home that I'd created with Xavier, and I began to build up the inward home within me.

Yes, I was emotionally abused. Yes, my parents' choices had shattered my early definition of love. Yes, I was a broken little girl in a grown woman's body. But God was still in control. He allowed everything to happen in my life to bring me to a point of surrender. He never left me. He never forsook me. He kept his loving hand over my life and preserved me not only for myself but for my daughters and for women across the world. I said yes to God in a way that I had never before, and he began the work of healing in my life. The time had come to yield it all and to love myself and God the way that he intended: with a love incorruptible.

Grace be with all who love our Lord Jesus Christ with undying and incorruptible love.

—Ephesians 6:24 AMP

"GOD OFTEN USES OUR DEEPEST PAIN AS THE LAUNCHING PAD OF OUR GREATEST CALLING."

–The Bible, Book of Romans

Epilogue

My Road to Recovery

God often uses our deepest pain as the
launching pad of our greatest calling.
—Romans 8:28

About nine years ago, I felt in my heart that I was to write a book through the eyes of a character named Brooklen. At that time, I figured the book would be about the perfect romance between this colorful character and her long-term love, Xavier. It'd be a story about their tumultuous ups and downs, but in the end they would run off into fairy tale land to live happily ever after. Boy, was I wrong. It wasn't until the repeated defects in my own relationship came to a head that I was given the ammunition to write the true story. Here are a few key lessons:

1. **God has a perfect plan.** Even though I made choices that missed the mark, he always brought me back on track to fulfill his intention for my life. Why? Because I am his child. You see, everyone has a story—some good, some bad, some ugly—and every story has a purpose. That purpose is to help others. When your heart is willing and open for God to use, then he will carry you through your story so that you can tell it. Your pain can be used for good, if you allow it.

2. **It was always about me.** My journey of enduring abuse and living in dysfunction led me to a place of self-reflection. I became hungry for

answers about why I was allowing myself to live a mediocre life when I knew I deserved more. My self-discovery journey allowed me to develop an incorruptible love for God and myself through the process of faith. The fears that had once controlled me no longer had power over me. I had been set free from childhood bondage, abuse, and insecurity. My work within this marriage was done, and it was time to move on. Greater things were waiting for me on the other side. It was through the troubles of this relationship that I discovered me.

3. **Self-care first.** Over the years, I had developed an unhealthy habit of denying my needs and excessively putting others before myself. I would never consider myself—in fact, I thought it was selfish to do so. I had to learn how to set healthy boundaries and to implement a regimen of self-care. Self-care can be whatever *you* want it to be. The point is to make sure you take this time for yourself daily. It will help replenish you for the duties ahead.

As I continued my healing process, I wanted to make sure that I filled my thoughts and time with activities that would benefit me. I had been worn down and sucked dry for the better part of my adult life, and it was time to fill myself back up. I set a challenge for myself and wrote out a bucket list to be completed in thirty days. I was intentional and urgent about my healing. I poured my energy and time into accomplishing this list. Now, I don't know where you are right now in your life, but a jolt of positive energy can do all of us some good no matter where we are. Whether you are celebrating a birthday, a divorce, or a new chapter in life, I'd like to challenge you to push yourself into your better future. I shared my list as an example.

Real Life
30-Day Bucket List

1. GIVE A PERSON IN NEED $35

2. GET MANI/PEDI

3. WRITE GRATITUDE NOTES/TEXTS TO MY CLOSET FRIENDS/FAMILY

4. CHANGE MY HAIR

5. DRINK MORE WATER

6. VOLUNTEER AT A PLACE FOR WOMEN

7. MEDITATE

8. JOG 3.5 MILES

9. RIDE A BIKE

10. 35 SQUATS 35 SIT UPS 35 PUSHUPS

11. READ PSALMS 35 – 35 TIMES

12. SAY A PRAYER WITH SOMEONE NEW

13. DO SOMETHING SCARY

14. TAKE A LONG, HOT BATH

15. FAST FOR 35 HOURS - NO SOCIAL MEDIA

16. TALK TO FINANCIAL ADVISOR

17. TAKE EACH DAUGHTER ON A DATE

18. SCHEDULE PHYSICAL AND MAMMOGRAM

19. FIND AND START COUNSELING

20. TAKE MYSELF ON A DATE

Now, use the following worksheet to write down your own thirty-day bucket list. In order to make this process even more memorable, take a photo every time you check something off the list. Capture your growth and use these photos as reminder of your personal freedom walk.

143

My 30-Day
Bucket List

1. _____
2. _____
3. _____
4. _____
5. _____
6. _____
7. _____
8. _____
9. _____
10. _____
11. _____
12. _____
13. _____
14. _____
15. _____
16. _____
17. _____
18. _____
19. _____
20. _____

#LoveIncorruptible

In closing, the journey for Brooklen Sapphire has barely scratched the surface. The former suppressed woman is reclaiming her identity and blazing a trail for others to find their personal freedom. Keep in mind that upon choosing freedom, there is a heavy requirement for internal dirty work to be done, but you don't have to go at it alone. You'll find that once you open your heart and mind, you'll start to find the resources necessary to get your healing. You'll start building better relationships with the people in your life. You'll attract the right supporters, the right therapists, the right books, and the right kind of fun for your personal walk. I hope that you take the sometimes uncomfortable yet critically necessary trip down memory lane to face your own giants and discover a love for yourself that can never be diminished—a love incorruptible. Go get your healing, and enjoy the ride!

One of the greatest rewards
is knowing that someone has been inspired
by my growing pains…

Acknowledgments

Love Incorruptible is the beginning of a lifelong process to identify, heal and love myself as a woman and mother in partnership with God. I thank all the characters in *Love Incorruptible* for the transformative lessons and their key contributions to my self-discovery journey.

To my father, the person that set the tone for love and relationships in my life – I appreciate you for who you are and your role to my growth. The dark void that I once perceived in my heart became the very thing I needed to find the light. God bless you.

To my mother, the thriving warrior. No matter how difficult the journey, you continue to persevere. You've taught me so much. I've learned to love and accept me, and as a result, I've learned to love and accept you. I forgave myself, and as a result, I have forgiven you. Thank you for your continued support.

To my sister, my best friend to the end and my secret keeper. The only person that knows every detail, heard every cry, listened to every story and still loves me the same. Thank you for being just perfect.

To my children, you inspire me to become the best version of myself, the God version! I have endured for you, loved for you, and now, I live for you. My baby queens, thank you for being your amazing little selves. The ceiling has been lifted. Now, soar!

To my tribe, you know who you are because I have expressed this to you vocally. Your part in this journey has been invaluable and impactful. Each of you, have changed my life for the better, and for that and so much more – I love you.

To my lessons in love – you played a necessary role in my story. What seemed painful then has lead me to destiny. Thank you.

To you reading this story, if you take anything away, please take the perfect concept of love – it never fails – in fact, love IS incorruptible! Learning to love yourself and God will carry you through to victory. Always forward!